New Jersey Noir: Cape May

NEW JERSEY NOIR:
CAPE MAY

A Novel

BY

William Baer

ABLE MUSE PRESS

Able Muse Press

www.ablemusepress.com

Printed in the United States of America

Library of Congress Control Number: 2019937303

ISBN 978-1-77349-033-5 (paperback)
ISBN 978-1-77349-034-2 (digital)

Cover image: "Just Wait" by Alexander Pepple

Cover & book design by Alexander Pepple

Able Muse Press is an imprint of *Able Muse: A Review of Poetry, Prose & Art* – at www.ablemuse.com

Able Muse Press
467 Saratoga Avenue #602
San Jose, CA 95129

For my family and friends—

especially Sam

CONTENTS

I

II

III

New Jersey Noir: Cape May

I

New Jersey has more laws than any other state, but a paucity of law-abiding citizens.

— Thomas C. Colt

1

Paterson, New Jersey

Tuesday, March 24th
42°

WANNA SEE some dead bodies?"

"How many?"

Yeah, yeah, I know. It sounds kind of callous, but when you've seen a billion stiffs, who cares about a few more?

Especially, if it's not your case.

"Six."

I was intrigued, ever so slightly, and Luca sensed it. He'd been my best friend since we were brats in grammar school, and he'd been kidding himself ever since that he could "read" me, that he could somehow "know" what I was thinking.

Well, maybe sometimes he could.

"You'll want to see this, Jack. I guarantee it."

Luca Salerno, former Paterson beat cop, was now the best detective working out of the Passaic County Courthouse in Paterson, New Jersey, and I knew what he was doing, and he knew that I knew what he was doing.

Trying to get me out of the house.

I was sitting in Stone House, my house, exactly a month after "the one whose name I dare not dwell on" jumped into her bright-red Neon and drove three thousand miles to California. It was also almost six weeks since my uncle was assassinated at the Paterson Falls, which was why the house was empty.

Except for me.

I stood up and looked out the back window of the house, which sits on top of Garrett Mountain, high above the nightlights of the city I loved, the city of Paterson. The city which, even though nobody knows it, made America the greatest country on earth. Yeah, the founders get some cred, and all the immigrants, and the much-praised "work ethic," etc., but Paterson blasted off the great American industrial juggernaut, being the home of our "second" revolution: industry/business.

It was one of the founders, of course, who kicked everything off. Who had the vision. Who looked at the awesome power of the falls and saw the nascent "engine" of the revolution. A guy named Hamilton. Soon the place was "Silk City," then it was "firearms" city, then it was "locomotive engines" city, then it was "aeronautics" city, with an awful lot of ups and downs along the way. Yeah, there's way too much crime in Paterson, too much corruption, too many fatherless households, too many botched educational schemes, but I still love the place.

I love the mountain, I love the river, I love the falls, I love the food, and I love the people.

I especially love the parades:

The African-American Day Parade, the Dominican Day Parade, the Turkish-American Day Parade, the Bangladeshi Day Parade, the Peruvian Day Parade, and all the other countless "ethnic day" parades. There's pretty much a new parade every week, which makes sense since Paterson is the most densely populated city in the US, excepting the big-boy across the Hudson, and the most ethnically diverse city in the US, excepting the same exception.

"You still there?" Luca wiseassed. "Or did the line go dead?"

I ignored his sarcasm, still staring at the glittering nightlights of the city which spread out before me. It was approaching midnight, and I'd been watching *Godfather II*, and I wasn't sure if I wanted to interrupt myself.

"Where?" I wondered.

"The riverbank. Off Totowa Ave."

I was still thinking.

"You'll enjoy it, Jack. I promise."

Hell, maybe I should get out of the house. I wasn't really sulking, and I certainly wasn't depressed, as a matter of fact, I've never been depressed in my life. It's not part of the family makeup. The genetic code. But after losing both my uncle and the pretty girl whom it's probably best not to think about, I was much enjoying the elemental pleasures: *The Godfathers I & II*, Faulkner, and Ross Macdonald.

Do private dicks really read books about private dicks?

Sure, they do.

Do mob guys really read books about the mob?

Sure, they do.

Do politician really read books about politicians?

Maybe.

Which, of course, assumes that they can read in the first place. Maybe they just watch the movies.

I do both.

Besides, nothing interesting had crossed my desk recently. These days I'm able to pick and choose my cases, but after the recent bloody mess, nothing interesting had walked into my office.

"You coming or not?"

Somebody was impatient.

"Sure," I said. "Why not?"

2

Cape May

YOUR NAME IS COLT (oddly enough).

You're a private investigator (even more oddly enough).

You come home (alone) from a dinner date with a pretty young woman at Tisha's on the Washington Mall. You pour yourself a brandy, a twelve-year-old Korbel, take off your clothes, fold them neatly on a leather chair, and go outside behind the house to your heated swimming pool. Why people have swimming pools a few blocks from the beach I have no idea, but I guess a heated pool makes a modicum of sense in the month of March.

You jump in, climb in, or dive in, then swish around for a while. You're thirty-eight years old, trim, attractive, competent, and likeable.

What are you thinking about?

Your past? Your future? Your job?

The difficult case you're working on?

Or maybe, probably, the pretty girl you took to Tisha's before dropping her off at her home on Beach Avenue.

The water's warm and intimate, the night's cool and brisk, the moonlight's soft and faint.

Not at all foreboding.

When you've had enough of its comforting wetness, you go to the ladder and rise from the pool. Did you sense something before it happened? Who knows? You're a private dick, and they all believe that they'll survive the darkness of the night and live to work the case another day.

Before you can reach for your white towel, waiting on a nearby deck chair, a figure appears in front of you, as if from nowhere, as if unthreateningly, then lifts a handgun of some kind and blows a tunnel through your forehead. You're dead, of course, before you hit the ground, before the bleeding starts, but, as for me, at that exact precise present moment, I know nothing about any of it.

3

The Waterfront

THE BEST is yet to come. . . ."

Yeah, I hope so.

Some Jersey guy named Sinatra was singing away, and I was wondering if it was true.

I was cruising my hyper-black Vsport, 410-hp twin-turbo XTS through the mean streets of Paterson heading for the Passaic River. Most of the good people were home and/or asleep, but disparate packs of loitering cretins still roamed the city streets.

Did I mention crime?

For a while, Camden got all the publicity. Newark too. But we've had more than our fair share. Then it got worse. Four years ago, the city ended up with a seventy-million-dollar budget deficit (don't get me started on that), and the town geniuses dealt with the "shortfall" by laying off 125 cops, which was about twenty-five percent of the total force, which was ridiculous.

Which naturally pumped up the crime stats.

Which was good for business if you were a private investigator.

Off Totowa Avenue, I pulled into Westside Park, parking next to Federici's World War I Monument, a good-looking Lady

Liberty. Then I strolled over to the riverbank, past some boys in blue, past some yellow crime-tape, past a couple of media parasites, and found Luca.

He nodded to his right, and I took a look.

He was right.

It *was* interesting.

There were six heads in a neat row on the riverbank staring rather wistfully at the endlessly flowing blackness of the Passaic River. It looked like they'd been buried in the ground with just their heads protruding, but I figured they were probably decaps.

"You promised 'bodies,'" I said.

Luca smiled.

He still had a small bandage over his throat where he'd been shot with an M24 sniper rifle four weeks ago. It put a bit more masculine gravel in his voice.

"We'll find them eventually."

(Meaning the bodies.)

"Your paisans?"

(Meaning the killers.)

"I'm thinking Peruvians."

"Why?"

He handed me a candy wrapper.

"We found it in a garbage can."

It was an empty bag of *Lantejas*. Very popular with the Peruvians.

Grageas de Pasta Sabor Chocolate Confitado.

"That sounds convenient."

"Too conveninent?"

I shrugged.

"Who found the heads?"

"Somebody called Joe Murphy at the *Herald* and told him to come over here. Somebody obviously wanted to make a statement."

Tomorrow, the six heads would be all over the news, and each and every one of the numerous ethnic mobs in Paterson would be thinking twice about expanding their turf.

Or messing with the Ravellos.

I took a closer look at the heads. An unhappy lot. It was hard to determine ethnicity in the mushy moonlight.

Maybe South America. Maybe Eastern European.

What difference did it make? No one would ever pin it on Don Ravello, and Luca knew it, and it infuriated him. He was a "good" Italian, and he hated the bad ones.

To distract himself, he decided to bust my balls.

"You keeping busy?"

I knew what he was doing.

"Yeah."

"That's not what Nonna says. She says you watch the two *Godfathers* over and over, back to back."

"You got something better to do?"

He was stumped.

"You need a case, Jack."

He was right.

Then Luca got called away by the ME, and I stood within the Paterson darkness and permitted myself to think about "her."

I pulled out my cell and read today's text. Then I reread her text from a month ago:

> Today I stopped at Niagara, stood at the falls, and thought about Sam Patch of Passaic Falls, New Jersey.

I smiled. What else could I do? A month ago, she was making her first "detour," as she headed back to California with Jersey still on her mind.

Back in 1827, some idiot named Sam Patch jumped off the Paterson Falls, also known as the Passaic Falls, and survived. When he discovered the next morning that he was instantly famous, he went up to Niagara, waved to all his "fans," kissed an American flag, and jumped 130 feet into the whirlpool below, surviving again. Then he went over to Rochester to jump the Genesee Falls. Which he did a second time, but this time, as the crowd stared ever so silently at the undisturbed surface of the river, there was no sign of Samuel Patch. Four months later, the illustrious "daredevil" was discovered frozen in the river-ice six miles from the falls.

Some people were saddened, of course, but most thought he was an idiot. Even Nathaniel Hawthorne wrote a piece about the "poor fellow" who'd thrown his life away "in pursuit of empty fame."

They put a makeshift wooden marker over his grave:

Here lies Sam Patch. Such is Fame.

Six months ago, when I told Roxanne (who was a committed Jerseyphile) the Sam Patch story, I managed to conjure up and recite one of the many old ditties about the Jersey daredevil.

She liked it a lot.

Poor Samuel Patch, a man once world renowned,
Much loved the water, and by it was drowned.
He sought for fame, and as he reached to pluck it,
He lost his ballast, then kicked the buck-it.

4

Stone Tower

Tuesday, March 24th
36°

W̶HAT HAPPENED?
      She woke up.
Were you wearing the stupid mask?
Yes.
A ski mask?
Yes.
Is that why you haven't been coming around lately?
Yes.
[Pause]
So what happened?
I took off the mask and told her everything.
Everything?
Yes.
That you'd been deceiving her, that you'd been stalking her, that you'd been coming into her house in the middle of the night just to be close to her?
    Yes.

That you loved her?

Yes.

What happened?

She left.

Left?

Yeah, she left for California.

In the middle of the night?

The next day.

What did she say?

When?

When she was still in the bed.

She said, "What's the matter with you?" And I said, "You." And she said, "Do you love me?" And I said, "Yes." And she said, "Do you want to marry me?" And I said, "Whatever you want."

Which was a pretty wimpy response.

If you weren't so blind, you could see me shrugging.

Keep going.

So she said, "When?" And I said, "Pick a day." And she thought about it for a moment.

A "moment"?

Yeah, she's the queen of snap judgments, and, oddly enough, most of them are good ones. Smart ones.

So what was her "judgment"?

Pretty much a "no."

Tell me.

She shook her head and said, "You're too messed up."

What did you say?

I agreed. Then she said, "I'd like a year to think about it."

No snap judgment there.

Nope.

Then she leaves the next day?

Yep.

Incommunicado for a year?

Not exactly. She came up with some guidelines.

Fill me in.

She said that we're each allowed one text, every day, one sentence long, and no "lovey" stuff.

She used the word "lovey"?

Yeah.

I've never sent a text.

Of course, you haven't. You're a billion years old, and you're blind as a bat.

Describe it.

It's like a short email, with a limit of 160 characters.

Including the spaces, I assume.

Including the spaces.

That's quite a romance you've got going there.

You got that right.

5

18 Marshall Street

THE SPEAKER came on.

"Am I interrupting the cannoli scene?"

It was Mrs. Doris Salerno, Luca's grandmother, who'd once run the office for my now-deceased uncle, who'd been, ever since Roxs took off for California, filling in at the reception desk.

I answered her question with a question.

"How do you know I'm not watching *GF II*?"

She didn't miss a beat. She never did.

"Am I interrupting the 'we wuz like the Romans' scene?"

I refused to respond.

It might seem strange to anyone living outside the boundaries of the beautiful Garden State, that such a loving self-sacrificing grandmother could also be such a perfect wiseass.

Welcome to New Jersey.

"You've got a potential client waiting in your luxurious waiting room. Mr. Richard O'Brien. Maybe he can get you up off your ass."

Mrs. S., Nonna, had once been a librarian. She'd also mothered and grandmothered the entire extended Salerno brood, and she always treated me and Luca like idiots. Like children. Even now.

"What does he want?" I wondered.

"It seems he believes that you can solve a crime. Remember them? When I asked him why, he said, 'Because he's supposed to be the best.'"

"Who could dispute that?"

Whether or not it was true, I'd picked up the "best" reputation two years ago when the governor's loco youngest daughter went missing, and I tracked her down inside the Pine Barrens. A few other cases also cemented my rep, and the recent ugly business with the so-called "Little Girl Killer" didn't hurt either. As a result, a parade of sadly desperate characters from all over the metro area, hoping against hope, tried to get through my door at 18 Marshall Street in downtown Paterson, two blocks from the courthouse, right across the street from the county jail.

I decided that the poor guy in the waiting room had suffered enough. Besides, *no one* ever got the upper hand with Luca's Nonna.

"Send him in."

He came through my office door, carrying a little leather briefcase, and unlike most of my other "visitors," he paid absolutely no attention to the surrounding office walls, covered with framed shots of NFL linebackers (I'd done a bit in the middle in high school) and all the legendary New Jersey singers.

Whitney, Sinatra, Springsteen, etc.

This guy was focused. He told me that he'd driven up from Cape May, which is about a two-and-a-half-hour drive, and I asked him why, and he told me.

"A murder." Then he corrected himself. "Two murders."

I was willing to listen.

"Have a seat."

He sat down, on the other side of my desk, as I unholstered my Python and put it on the desk in front of him. It was my habit to make my clients nervous, to make them fully aware that I was serious, dead and deadly serious, and, of course, there was no more effective means of intimidation than the appearance of a Colt Python, the most accurate handgun in the world, the best all-around handgun in the world, given to me by my uncle when I was twelve years old.

Created, of course, by the Colts.

It's deep royal blue, double-action, hyper-masculine, hyper-affirmative, and just like the old Revolution flag with the coiled snake that said "Don't Tread on Me," this particular python said, without equivocation, "Don't F-Around with Me."

Luca Salerno was my best friend, but my Colt Python was my second best friend.

O'Brien didn't seem bothered by the gun at all. Maybe it reassured him. He wanted help, and he sat there and stared at me like a supplicant high-school student.

Are you wondering what the guy looked like?

Like a smaller Liam Neeson, maybe six foot, certainly not six-six, without the classic Neeson "edge," wearing a blue-tinted dress shirt, tieless, with a preppy navy sports coat. Maybe fifty-five, nicely preserved, with that casual and unpretentious air of money and distinction.

It was a longtime habit.

One that was very helpful in my line of work. It was something that my uncle and I had started doing when I was still a kid, long before I went off to Rutgers to become the only nascent PI in the history of the world who double-majored in philosophy and cinema. So we started using the entire Hollywood "roster," the wide range of Hollywood stars, to describe our clients, witnesses, snitches, thugs, etc. This one looks a bit like Bob Mitchum. This one looks a bit like the young Maureen O'Hara. This one "wishes" he looks like James Dean. Etc. Since the old man (my uncle) knew his films almost as well as me, we used the entire scope of Hollywood history, from the silents right to the present.

So this one looked a little bit like Liam Neeson, without the "particular set of skills."

That was *my* job.

"How can I help?"

Amazingly, he told me that some guy named Edward Colt, who was apparently some kind of PI down in Cape May, had gotten himself shot to death last night in his own backyard.

"Are you related?" he wondered.

"Never heard of him. Are you sure he's a PI?"

I thought I knew every private dick in New Jersey. I also thought I knew every "Colt" in New Jersey.

"I'm sure. I hired him nine days ago to look into a cold case involving my daughter. Now he's dead, and I'm suspicious that the murders are related."

Which seemed feasible. But I was still baffled by this now-dead Colt character.

"How long was he working in Cape May?"

"Just a few months. Before that he worked in Pennsylvania. In Harrisburg. With good references."

"Tell me about the cold case."

It was perfectly obvious that *that's* why O'Brien was really here.

"My daughter was murdered ten years ago. She was seventeen at the time."

"Tell me about it."

"She was out with some friends, vanished for a day, then someone saw her car driving across the beach into the ocean near the Cove Beach jetty. They found her dead in the trunk of the car."

I remembered it. Some of it. It got a lot of press.

Naturally, the water and the trunk made me think of *The Killing*. That "Who Killed Rosie Larson?" television series that I'd watched when it first aired on AMC.

I wondered if one inspired the other.

"She had a twin, right?"

"Yes, but her sister wasn't there that night."

I was intrigued.

Definitely.

Luca said that I "needed" a case.

"Tell me about yourself."

"I'm a judge at the Cape May County Courthouse. Mostly divorce-case arbitration. I've lived in Cape May my whole life, and I'm divorced myself, living with my daughter."

I liked the guy, so I told him that I'd come down to Cape May and look into it.

He was relieved, grateful.

"There's something else," he said.

I waited.

"Two days ago, Colt came to my house and gave me the key to his office and a copy of his will, which he'd recently drawn up. For some reason, the will left me all of his money and all of his office files."

"Why?"

"I don't know. I was very uneasy about it, and I certainly don't need the man's money, but he said that he'd become 'obsessed' with my daughter's cold case and that he wanted it solved, regardless of whatever might happen to him."

"Did he think he was in danger?"

"He didn't act like it."

"How well did you know him?"

"I hardly knew him at all. We met a couple of times about the case. That was it."

"Didn't he have any family?"

"His mother died recently. I never heard about anyone else."

"So you went along with it?"

"I did. I tried to discourage him, but he insisted, and I relented. I had no idea that he'd be dead the next day."

O'Brien opened his briefcase, pulled out a bunch of files, and put them on my desk.

"When I heard he was shot last night, I immediately went to his office and got his files. There wasn't much. He'd only been working the case for nine days. Then I found this."

He put a healthy stack of bills on my desk.

"It was in one of the files. It's twenty-five thousand dollars."

The bills had a yellow Post-it attached, so I picked up the twenty-five thousand and read the note:

Remittance for Jack Colt.

I looked back at the judge.

"He wants *you* to solve the case," he said. Then he corrected himself, "*Both* cases."

When O'Brien was gone, I entered my uncle's dimly lit office and stuffed the cash in the safe. The room was full of books and files and documents, but it was empty, and I sat down on the top of the desk. Tom Colt, who was actually my great-uncle, had been the most important person in my life, raising me after the death of my parents in a car crash thirty-one years ago. In truth, Tom Colt was the *best* private dick in the metro area, and he'd taught me everything I knew. The only thing he'd never taught me was how to deal with a life without him.

I'll have to figure that out on my own.

I'm not a brooder, and the Colts certainly aren't sentimentalists, but we're human, and I miss him a lot. So I shifted focus and thought about Roxs, which he wouldn't have minded at all. Two short months ago, the "boss" was working away in his office, right here in this room, and Roxs was sitting out in the waiting room at the reception desk. Life, despite all of its natural crap, was good. Very good. But now he was dead and buried in Cedar Lawn Cemetery, and Roxs was back home in California, Hermosa Beach, three thousand miles away, trying to figure me out.

Good luck with that.

Last night, just before I left Stone Tower, the old Jesuit asked me, "What'll she do?"

Meaning, "When her year of 'thinking it over' is over, what do you think she'd decide, 'yes' or 'no'?"

I told him what I thought.

"No."

Why *should* she want me? As a matter of fact, why should *any* woman want any man, period, given our self-absorption and barbaric behavior?

I stood up and looked at myself in the mirror.

Tom Colt was never vain like his nephew, but he was always neat and meticulous and professional, and he never left the office without checking himself out.

I stared at the creep in the mirror.

He was thirty-two years old, trim, a tough guy, six foot two, and, essentially, in your face. He was wearing one of his two-dozen identical black Armani suits, with one of his three-dozen identical navy button-downs, with one of his four-dozen thin black ties.

I couldn't see the color of his eyes, which are dark-dark brown, because, all of the day and all of the night, he wears Lightforce shades from Ray-Ban. The Colts are pretty much immune to the cold and the heat, but they're "light sensitive." Whatever that means.

Even in the dimly shadowed lights of the room, I could see the never-discussed, one-inch "cross" scar in the smack-dab center of his forehead. As for his hair, it was thick, the blackest black, and slicked-and-greased back like a Jersey guido.

I looked at myself.

As objectively as I could.

I looked like some kind of a mob flunky. The scary kind. The one you don't want to run into in a dark alley. I tried to imagine meeting myself in a dark alley, but it didn't work. I was too cocky to be spooked by myself.

Back to the fundamental question: how could a woman, *any* woman, want a piece of that?

Especially a fun-loving California volleyball-playing beach girl. (What the hell *is* volleyball anyway?)

But it wasn't just me. How could *any* woman want *any* man?

I thought of that scene in Bergman's *Smiles of a Summer Night*. Gunnar Björnstrand (the greatest actor in film history, by the way, and my own particular favorite) has just fallen into a puddle, so his ex-lover, the lovely Eva Dalbeck, gives him a ridiculous nightshirt and an even more ridiculous night cap (with a tassel no less). Then she leads him over to a mirror to show him how silly he looks, and Björnstrand makes no attempt to duck the issue:

"How could a woman ever love a man?"

Good question.
Then he wonders out loud:

"Can you tell me that?"

Dalbeck explains:

"A woman's view is seldom based on aesthetics."

Exactly.
Another woman's voice suddenly squawked out from the speaker on the desk in the next room.
"Did he leave a retainer?"
She was busting my balls again.
"Yeah, twenty-five thousand dollars."
I thought that might shut her up.
"Is that all?"

6
Appendix I

LAST WILL AND TESTAMENT OF EDWARD J. COLT

I, EDWARD J. COLT, a thirty-eight-year-old adult residing at 921 Benton Avenue, Cape May, New Jersey, being of sound mind, declare this to be my Last Will and Testament. I revoke all previous wills and codicils.

ARTICLE I
I APPOINT RICHARD O'BRIEN as my Personal Representative to administer this Will, and ask that he be permitted to serve without Court supervision and without posting bond.

ARTICLE II
I DIRECT MY PERSONAL REPRESENTATIVE to pay out of my residuary estate all the expenses of my last illness, funeral expenses, a suitable marker for my grave, administration expenses, all legally enforceable creditor claims, all federal estate taxes, state inheritance taxes, and all other governmental charges imposed by reason of my death.

ARTICLE III

I DEVISE, BEQUEATH, and give the entirety of my estate, including my business files and records, to Richard O'Brien.

ARTICLE IV

SHOULD THE BENEFICIARY not survive me by thirty days, his bequeathment shall be distributed to his surviving daughter.

Edward J. Colt [signature]

SELF-PROVING AFFIDAVIT

THIS INSTRUMENT WAS SIGNED and acknowledged by Testator as his Last Will and Testament in our presence, and we, at his request, and in his presence, and in the presence of each other, have subscribed our names as witnesses. Under penalties for perjury, we, the undersigned Testator and witnesses declare:

1. That the Testator executed this instrument as his Will;

2. That in the presence of witnesses, the Testator signed this Will;

3. That the Testator executed the Will as his free and voluntary act;

4. That the Testator was of sound mind.

WITNESS: *Lloyd Harrison* [signature]
WITNESS: *Julie Lennox* [signature]

7

Stone Tower

Wednesday, March 25th
41°

W*HO THE HELL'S Edward Colt?*
Asked Monsignor John C. Colt, old-school renegade Jesuit, canon lawyer, and the uncle of my great uncle Tom, thus making him my great-great-uncle.

He wasn't really mad, he was just baffled.

He was also a ninety-eight-year-old "hellologist," who'd written over thirty-five highly regarded theological treatises, including a book on Gehenna that made Dante look like a walk in the park. It was dedicated to me, apparently intended to keep me on the straight and narrow.

For much of my adult life, he was off at the Vatican, either running the place or raising havoc, depending on which version you believed. Now he was back in New Jersey, blind as a bat, frail, ready to die, and attempting to serve as my moral compass, my Jiminy Cricket. He was, even now, well connected in Paterson, and the mayor and the bishop got him back into his old quarters, the room at the top of the Lambert Tower, sitting on a rise on Garret Mountain overlooking Lambert Castle.

Yeah, Paterson has a castle.

(Doesn't every US city?)

It was built by Catholina Lambert, the textile baron, back in 1892, and now it's a historical monument. The high stone tower was built nearby, with a panoramic view of Paterson below, which, of course, the old blind priest could no longer see. Maybe Lambert built the tower so he could see the mobs of union thugs coming up the mountain like the townspeople at the end of *Frankenstein*.

(I made that up.)

Tonight, the little man was standing at the little window of his elevated priestly cell, staring out at nothing.

Tell me.

I've got no idea. I never heard of him. I thought I knew all the New Jersey Colts.

Me, too.

(Beat)

He got himself shot to death last night in Cape May, so I'm heading down there to check it out.

You'll miss the city.

Meaning Paterson. It was no secret that I wasn't much of a traveler.

Actually, I'm looking forward to it. A bit like Nicholson in *The Pledge*, when he moves into the small town to try and solve an unsolved murder. I always liked that premise.

Which means you didn't like the execution.

Exactly. I never liked how he used the little girl as bait, and I thought the ending was deus ex machina.

(Beat)

You ever see it?

The last film I saw was Babette's Feast. *A great film.*

A great film.

Then I gave up filmwatching.
Why?
Someone was sick, so I offered it up.
Who was sick?
You.
I've never been sick in my life. Not *that* sick.
You were back then.
When was *Babette's*? 1988?
1987.
I was five back then.
And burning with a fever.
[Pause]
Thanks.
Don't mention it.

8

Riverfront Park

Wednesday, March 25th
38°

I T WAS A LOVELY DAY, much less lonely than the rest.

But now the day is done, and you're staring across the dark Susquehanna towards City Island and the distant Blue Mountain. Since it's the middle of the night, Blue Mountain looks black.

The park is empty and comforting.

Its views, as always, are lovely.

You've *never* felt vulnerable here at Riverfront Park.

All your vulnerabilities lie within your heart.

Earlier, you'd spent a wonderful day with little Emily, your sister's ten-year-old, at Hersheypark. Then Chocolate World. What in the world could be more marvelous, at *any* age, than something called Chocolate World?

In the morning, you'd "done" the park, riding, it seemed, half of its seventy rides, excepting, of course, the roller coasters, which you, not your little niece, had chickened out of. After an hour or so at the zoo, you spent another hour or so at the Boardwalk Waterpark. In the afternoon, after lunch, it was time for Chocolate World: the Trolley Works, the Chocolate Tour, and the "Create-Your-Own Candy Bar" experience.

Surprisingly, Emily seemed to enjoy the afternoon even more than the morning, learning how chocolate was made, making her own chocolate bar, and hearing about the visionary life of the amazing Milton Hershey.

On the ten-mile drive back to Harrisburg, Emily fell asleep, in an obvious state of somnambulant bliss. Eventually, you carried the little angel from the front seat of your Equinox to her mother's waiting arms. Then you went back to your perfect and perfectly empty townhouse condo, near Market Square, unable to sleep, wishing that *you* had an Emily.

A child.

Wishing also, at thirty-five, that you had a man.

A reliable one.

Wishing that you had *someone*.

Forbes Magazine had once described Harrisburg as the second best place in America to "raise a family." Which was meaningful only if you actually *had* a family.

Or at least some prospects.

So you did what you've always done when you wanted to "think," even if it would prove to be a perfectly useless and self-defeating kind of thinking. You quickly re-dressed, threw on your burgundy trench, and strolled down to the park. To the very same bench where you used to sit with *him*, watching the magnificent evening suns setting across the river, as lovers and others strolled the walkway over the Walnut Street Bridge from City Island.

Tonight, right now, you were doing your very best *not* to feel sorry for yourself. Doing your very best to think about little

Emily and all her chocolate smiles and all the marvelous wonders of the day now past.

Then you "sense" something.

You look up.

You see the dark, imposing, unrecognizable figure standing above you, having appeared, it seems to you, from nowhere, from deep within the most mysterious darkness of the silent night. At first, you're more surprised than frightened, although you're not sure why, as you stare at the figure as it stares at you. It seems as though it's trying to figure something out.

As if trying to comprehend the incomprehensible.

Spooked, you're just about to say something when the gun rises in front of your face and fires, and you can remember nothing else.

Never again.

You slump.

You fall off the bench, down to the ground, fortuitously dead before the thirty-two ounces of Drano are slowly poured over your once-pretty face, seeping into your dead lifeless eyes, into your slightly open mouth, still slightly surprised.

9

Congress Hall

I WAS SITTING on the dark empty beach behind Congress Hall. I'd already read today's text, and I was rereading her text from a month ago.

Her second "detour":

> *I'm now in South Bend, ignoring the Golden Dome, the stadium, the basilica, and the Grotto, standing in front of the Purcell Pavilion booing the naughty Irish girls.*

I smiled.

Generally, I didn't smile that much, but the California beach girl often made me smile. I tried to picture her, standing there, all alone, like a complete idiot, in front of the sports pavilion, booing the venue.

I knew why, of course. Three years ago when she was captain of the Pepperdine volleyball team, they'd traveled to Indiana, lost a close one, and then, after the game, a couple of the Irish girls were "rude."

"They dissed us."

Which is why they were "naughty," a word not much used in the current twenty-first century.

I stared out at the ocean, dark and deadly. At its forty-one-million square miles, over the Gulf Stream, into the far dark Atlantic, into the North American Gyre, into the calm unfathomable depthlessness and blue-black mystery of the Sargasso Sea.

Thinking of Augustine:

> *Men go abroad to wonder at the heights of mountains, at the tremendous waves of the sea, the long courses of the rivers, at the vast compass of the ocean, at the circular motions of the stars, and they pass by themselves without wondering.*

I was trying not to pass myself by, but I wasn't sure how well I was doing.

Earlier, after a pleasant drive down the parkway to Exit Zero (Cape May), I'd gone over to Colt's office on Perry Street, which was mostly empty and worthless. There was a small, rather sad sign on the front door beneath his name that read:

> *Solving Crimes Is My Business.*

Then I drove over to Congress Hall, went up to the "Grant Room" on the third floor, quickly changed into my black sweats and Nikes, and read over the files.

They weren't much help either:

> *Some old newspaper articles about the cold case.*
>
> *His notes on his two interviews (no tapes or videos).*
>
> *Crime scene photos.*

Suspect photos.

The forensic report on the car pulled from the ocean.

The autopsy report.

*Photos of the dead body, her clothes, and the contents of
her purse and wallet, containing the usual stuff—
cash, credit cards, cosmetics, etc., as well as:*

A B&B business card for the Gingerbread House.

A 4/8 service station receipt.

There was also a typed "suspect list" with the last two
names added in pencil and the name "Sehorn" penciled in after
"Rockingham":

Ronnie Miller – victim's best friend, age 18

Isabella (Izzy) Borelli – victim's friend, age 16

Rita Rockingham Sehorn – victim's friend, age 15

Billy ?? – Johns Hopkins student, age 18?

"Sonny" ?? – University of Maryland student, age 18?

Judge Richard O'Brien – victim's father, age 42

Rikki (Erica) O'Brien – victim's twin sister, age 16

Tommy Garrison – victim's boyfriend, age 17

Kitty Walsh O'Brien – victim's mother, age 34

Mitchell Kain – witness on the beach, age 48

I looked closely at the names, and I was surprised to see one that I knew. Rita Sehorn. A prosecutor at the Newton Courthouse in North Jersey. I'd met her once at some lawyer "thing" at the Brownstone in Paterson, and when she seemed interested, I mingled back into the crowd.

I pulled out her "suspect" photo. It was definitely Rita, ten years younger.

Isabella's last name "Borelli" also seemed vaguely familiar, with, it seemed to me, some kind of Paterson connection. But Izzy's picture set off no alarms, so maybe her last name was just a coincidence. But it was hard to ignore that stupid little dog, a Yorkshire terrier, she was holding in her photo. I looked closely at the little handwritten note attached to her picture. It said, "missing," so I immediately texted Nonna, who was sleeping in her warm bed in Paterson, and told her to find out where Izzy Borelli was living these day, using the dog. People often get addicted to breeds, and I was betting that Izzy, wherever the hell she was, had a terrier sleeping at the foot of her bed.

There were also a bunch of happy photos of the four girls who were together that afternoon and evening before one of them went missing. Pretty young high school girls, full of life and dreams and girly smiles, having fun in their hometown, near their beautiful beach, until one of them ended up dead in the trunk of her submerged car.

The prettiest one.

I now knew the basics of the case. What the cops knew back then, and what Edward Colt knew two days ago before he was shot in the head:

It was ten years ago, on a Thursday, on an unseasonably warm April day (4/7). Nikki Nicole O'Brien (the vic) and three of her closest girlfriends (Ronnie Miller, Rita Rockingham, and Isabella Morelli) met two young college boys (Billy and Shawn, last names unknown) on the Cape May promenade. The boys had stopped in Cape May on the way home from Maryland, heading for North Jersey (specifics unknown). Earlier, the girls had attended an afternoon baseball game at a local Cape May high school. They met the boys around 3:30, went bowling at Shoreline Lanes, picked up some take-out food, then hung out near the Cape May Lighthouse, on the nearby "Hawk Watch." They did a little light drinking, no drugs, and had a good time. Around seven o'clock, Nikki got a text, and she asked Ronnie (who was driving the girls) to drop her off at her home. Then the two guys decided to leave for North Jersey.

The victim's identical twin sister, Rikki O'Brien, wasn't there that day or evening since she'd had EMT training at 5:00. After her training session, she went home, did some homework, and spent the evening with her father.

Late that Thursday night, Nikki called her sister and told her that she (along with Ronnie) would be spending the next two nights at the home of the twin's aunt (Kathleen O'Brien, now deceased) in Diamond Beach, north of Cape May. This raised no alarms, as the twins often helped out their elderly aunt. Two nights later, at approximately 3:55 a.m., an astonished dog-walker on the Cape May promenade saw a yellow Mustang inexplicably gliding across the beach toward the jetty near the Sunset Pavilion. Then disappear into the ocean. He called 911.

When the car was pulled on the beach, the drowned body of Nikki O'Brien was found inside the trunk of her car.

Four pretty high school girls having some innocent fun with a couple of "traveling through" college boys. For some reason, something about it reeked of jealousy. Not the "green-eyed monster" of *Othello*, but the pathological sexual jealousy of *Cymbeline* and *The Winter's Tale*.

Maybe I was getting way ahead of myself.

Maybe not.

I looked at the ocean again.

I was sitting on my windbreaker, on top of the cool March-hardened sand.

Yeah, I'm a city boy, but the ocean's like a car crash or a fistfight or a fire or a parade—you can't take your eyes off it. You stand there, or you sit there, and you just stare into its mesmerizing depthless black infinity, which somehow makes you comfortable with death, with termination, with your own insignificance.

Enough of that.

I was facing a long day tomorrow, and I knew that I should get up off my ass and go back to my room, but I was enjoying the night and the solitude. Earlier, when I checked in at Congress Hall, the concierge told me that something called the Travel Channel, whatever that is, had once decided that Cape May was one of America's "top ten" beaches. Not just in New Jersey, which has countless great beaches, but in *all* of the US.

Of course, the Travel Channel people meant during the daytime, but I was never a lie-in-the-sun type of guy, and I preferred my beaches in the dead of night, preferably in the dead of winter.

March would do nicely.

Cape May sat at the extreme southern end of the state, at the southern end of 141 miles of beautiful New Jersey beaches known collectively as the Jersey Shore. The town was ridiculously "pretty," chock full of quaint Victorian homes, many of them now serving as B&Bs. As a matter of fact, little Cape May had more old Vic homes than any other place in the United States, except for San Francisco, which was a hell of a lot bigger. Our dearly beloved federal government, rather than go through the interminable hassle of designating *all* of the old homes as National Historical Landmarks, made the entire damn town a National Historical Landmark, making it the only town so designated in the entire country.

I have to admit that I'm a Jersey tough guy, but I can also appreciate "pretty" stuff like beaches and houses, but I'm much more interested in the history, and Cape May was overloaded with that. It was the first seaside resort in America (disputed sometimes by Long Beach, NJ), and the first resort to have a boardwalk. Back in the nineteenth century, it was flush with famous visitors. Presidents Pierce, Buchanan, Grant, and Arthur all stayed at Congress Hall, and Benjamin Harrison made it his official Summer White House. Even Lincoln's supposed visit back in 1849 was followed by all kinds of various celebrities like Stephen Decatur, George Meade, General Sherman, Lily Langtry, John Philip Sousa, Clara Barton, and Oscar Wilde.

Some claim that Cape May was discovered by Henry Hudson in 1609, but all the rest of us, including every single New Jersey Italian, believe that it was discovered by the Florentine, Giovanni da Verrazzano, in 1524, when he was sailing *La Dauphine* up the East Coast under the French flag. When he spotted a lovely cape and called it *Bonvietto*, which was certainly Cape May.

I took a last look at the ocean.

It was time to solve a murder.

Two of them.

10

The Lobster House

Thursday, March 26th
48°

I WONDERED IF you'd show up."

Which was one of the benefits (or detriments) of being famous. Being recognized.

Dawson was sitting in the far corner table of the Raw Bar at the Lobster House on Fisherman's Wharf, sitting beneath a mounted helmsman's wheel, behind a graveyard of crustacean limbs and two glass-mugs of a dark brown beer.

One mostly empty, one full.

He seemed as happy as a man could be happy.

Nick Dawson was the detective lead on the Edward Colt murder. He wore jeans, a cheap black blazer, and no tie. He looked like a rough-around-the-edges Irishman, approaching forty or so, and he didn't seem at all irritated that I'd popped up from nowhere.

"You related?" he wondered.

"I've never heard of the guy."

Dawson was surprised, maybe even disappointed, but *nothing* was about to interfere with or undermine the ecstasy of his culinary engagements.

"Grab a seat, and get some grub. It's right from the sea this morning. The best seafood in the universe, and the beer's just as good."

He thought things over, with an almost profound musing.

"I love beer," he assured me.

I had no reason to disbelieve him, but I hated beer, seldom drank at all, and found seafood, particularly arthropods, absolutely revolting. Especially the smell. Yeah, I know, I guess I'm in the minority, but I eat nothing from the sea, limiting my carnivorous activities to cattle, lambs, hogs, and a few chickens.

My uncle believed that the reason for my revulsion was the open-air fish markets in Paterson when I was a kid. You could smell them a mile away, and they were anything but appetizing.

Maybe he was right.

I sat down and watched Dawson eat. It was a courtesy call. I didn't want him to hear that I was in town snooping around in his case, and I wanted to assure him that I'd keep out of his way.

I also wanted to see what he knew.

Which was next to nothing.

"The guy was a ghost," he assured me.

"What about Harrisburg?"

"He only lived there a short time, did a few nothing-much cases, and seems to have made no friends."

"What about before that?"

"Nothing."

"Nothing?"

"Nothing."

"What about his mother? Didn't he go to her funeral a few weeks ago?"

"Supposedly. He definitely left town, but no one seems to

know where he went. I've got somebody pinging his cell right now, maybe we can get a location."

"Can you let me know?"

"Sure."

He took an Irish swig, more of a gulp, of the dark-dark beer, and tried to explain himself.

"I'm not the proprietary type. I'm glad you're down here, Colt, and I'm ready to share."

"I appreciate it."

Which was true.

"What about the old case?"

"*The Killing* killing?"

"Yeah."

"I was a beat cop back in those days. You need to talk to Helen Pavese."

"I'm planning on it."

I was also hoping that the stink of the place wouldn't cling to my Armani suit. Otherwise, I'd have to burn it on the beach tonight.

"Any rumors?" I wondered.

He knew exactly what I meant.

"Not really. Most of the suspicion came down on the college kids, especially Billy."

"Why Billy?"

"Because he and Nikki were apparently eyeing each other. Flirting around, like kids do. But he's long long gone, and so's the other one."

"You think it was a rationalization back then? The easy way out?"

He seemed confused, so I clarified.

"It's pretty easy to drop the rap on a kid who's gone. Who's completely out of the picture. Who's a mystery."

"Yeah, could be. Maybe."

We swapped cards, and I stood up, quickly escaping from the old boat house. I went outside and sat at a table on the wharf overlooking the Cape May harbor, checking Nonna's report.

Roxanne Faulkner was the best researcher I'd ever known, but she was now in sunny California. But Mrs. S. had been a librarian most of her life, and she also enjoyed snooping around for info:

> *Richard O'Brien (age 52, judge):*
>
> *He's quite the big deal in Cape May's divorce court, with a reputation as an effective "arbiter," with a reputation for "fairness." He went to Rutgers undergrad, then Rutgers-Camden Law. He seems the bookish thoughtful scholarly type, apparently quite pleasant (just as he was when he came to the office) and easy to get along with. Twenty-seven years ago, he married a pretty young girl (Kitty Walsh) from the Pine Barrens when she was barely seventeen. A year later, almost immediately after the twins (Rikki and Nikki) were born, she left and returned to the Pines. They divorced two years later, and she seems to have had nothing to do with raising the girls. As the tenth anniversary of his daughter's death was approaching, O'Brien hired Edward Colt to look into the ten-year-old cold case. You know what happened then.*
>
> *I hope you're behaving yourself down there, eating lots of slimy seafood, and wearing sunblock.*
>
> *Love, Nonna*

11

Reading Beach

I HOPED YOU'D SHOW UP."

Another benefit of being famous.

Actually a detriment:

High expectations.

We were standing on the upper-level porch of her huge house, staring across Beach Avenue at the Atlantic Ocean.

Helen Pavese was mid-fifties, early retirement, most probably a local beach girl turned cop. The Jersey sun had burned some age into her face, and she had that "divorced more than once" look, but she was definitely pretty once upon a time. I'd say she was a Helen Mirren type. She held her daiquiri like she'd held way too many of them, but she was still deeply concerned about the case that she'd never been able to solve.

I knew it was rude, but I asked anyway:

"How can you afford a place like this?"

"I've lived here my whole life. It was my grandfather's."

She definitely didn't mind my question, and she wasn't ashamed to be the beneficiary of Cape May money.

She looked at the beach, mostly deserted on a March afternoon. Then she and her daiquiri tried to explain herself.

"When I was a kid I loved mysteries, but I failed to solve the first one I tried to solve."

I waited.

"William Kidd."

Everybody in New Jersey knew the rumors about Captain Kidd and his treasures. A lot of people were convinced that he buried most of his booty at the Jersey Shore before he got himself arrested in Boston, tried in London, and hung from a rope on Execution Dock in 1701. After which, they suspended his decomposing body over the Thames for three years to discourage would-be pirates.

"I thought it was Brigantine?" I remembered.

"There's other evidence that he buried on the cape."

I guess she never found it.

"But I'll tell you something, Jack Colt, I'd rather solve the Nikki O'Brien case than find all of Kidd's treasures."

I believed her.

"You want a drink?"

She wanted company.

"I'm working."

She understood, and she sat down in a chair, and I did the same, both facing the ocean.

"Ask me anything."

I did.

"What about the 'lost' day?"

"I have no idea where she was. It's always driven me nuts."

"What about Diamond Beach?"

"She definitely lied to her sister about going up to her aunt's place, and she got her best pal Ronnie to cover for her."

"What about the B&B card?"

"Rikki told me that the Gingerbread House was their favorite B&B in town, even though they'd never been inside. When I checked the register, she'd never been there."

"Was the gas tank full when they pulled the car out of the ocean?"

She seemed surprised.

"Yeah, mostly. Almost."

"Edward Colt had a typed 'suspect list' in his files. Are you the one who typed it up?"

"Yes. I gave him a copy when he stopped by to see me last week."

"Did he ask any interesting questions?"

"Not really. Mostly generic. He was very polite, very conscientious, but I have to admit, I didn't have much confidence that he'd figure things out."

She added:

"Unlike you."

I ignored it.

"Who was your prime suspect?"

"The boyfriend. Tommy Garrison. Let's face it, the kid's girlfriend was off flirting with some college boy, and no high school kid's going to like the sound of that. But we had nothing on him."

"Why was Nikki's father on your suspect list?"

She shook her head, as if at her own foolishness.

"Oh, that was just my natural cynicism at work. Richard O'Brien seemed too good to be true. He still does. But when I checked him out, there was nothing. *Nothing*. I wondered if there might have been some disgruntled plaintiff out there, harboring a grudge, but I checked out all his cases, talked to every divorcée/

divorcé in the county, and came up with nothing. The guy's clean as a whistle. So were the twins."

"What about the sister?"

(Meaning, what about sororicide?)

Pavese laughed.

"Nah, no way."

"It happens."

(Meaning that siblings sometimes kill their siblings.)

"Yeah, but not those two, not the Bobbsey twins, the nerd sisters, the Stepford twins. It would have been like killing herself."

"Which people do."

"Which people do."

12

Cinco de Mayo

Thursday, March 26th
48°

I LOOKED OUT the window, across Route 109, watching the EMT truck, with flashers off, pull into the marina parking lot.

Louise Brooks got out.

The side of the truck said "Cape May Emergency," next to one of those big blue Stars of Life. She was dressed, meticulously, in EMT white pants, cute blue Nikes with orange laces, and an immaculate EMT white blouse with red circular patches on each sleeve.

I was finishing up the last of my three tortillas, the remnant of my entomatadas platter, sitting inside the lively colored, not-really-that-tacky Cinco de Mayo restaurant, with appropriate mariachi playing in the background. She wasn't *really* Louise Brooks, of course, but she had the same dark cropped hair that Brooks had made famous over a hundred years ago, especially in Pabst's sexually creepy *Pandora's Box*. Her haircut became the cut *de choix* of the twenties flappers, including other huge stars like Clara Bow and Colleen Moore. It's known, both then and now, as a "bob," as in Fitzgerald's famous story "Bernice Bobs Her Hair."

There've been many subsequent bobs over the years, and numerous modified bobs, of course, (see Mireille Mathieu, Liza's Sally Bowles, Fiorentino in *Men in Black*, Thurman in *Pulp Fiction*, etc.), but this one was called a "shingle" bob, with dead-perfect bangs across the forehead, with the hair on the sides coming forward a bit onto the cheek.

Naturally, I wondered if she'd still have the bob since I'd seen the photos of the twins last night, but that was ten years ago, and maybe things had changed. They hadn't. She looked exactly the same. Tallish (almost six foot), thin, trim, athletic, with pale but perfect Irish skin, brown eyes (which I knew from the photos), high cheekbones, and a red-red mouth that seemed unintentionally provocative.

But was.

She was kind of perfect.

Perfectly adorable. (Can men say that about a woman anymore? Who knows? Screw it.) She was, of course, a carbon copy of her dead twin sister, and both of them looked a bit like Roxanne, which was why I'd pushed their images out of my mind last night in the Grant Room.

Great!

I'd gotten myself duped into solving the murder of a girl who looked too much like the girl who'd just left me, with the dead girl's identical still running around town and, apparently, looking for me.

She crossed the road, entered the restaurant, and walked right up to my table at the front window. I felt like I wanted to spend the rest of my life with her. Yeah, I know it's a perfectly stupid thing to say, especially since I've been doing some moaning-and-groaning about the California girl, but underneath the hardass exterior, I'm just a "regular" guy (remember the jackass in the mirror?), and this pretty girl could make Dante forget Beatrice Portinari.

I looked up.

She looked down.

Most intelligent human beings are wary of the likes of me, even sitting in a Mexican restaurant with a warm tortilla in my hand. Most people simply turn around and walk in the other direction, and, if that's impossible, they tread ever so lightly. But this one seemed perfectly as ease. Maybe patching up all her car crash victims and strokes and heart failures—all the intubations, cricothyrotomies, and defibrillations—had made her comfortable with just about anything.

Even me.

She looked right through my Ray-Ban shades.

"John Colt?"

She knew who I was.

"You know who I am."

She was unfazed.

"I have a few questions."

She wasn't angry. She wasn't even aggressive or demanding. She simply had "a few questions."

I liked her voice. It was calm, comforting, lower than expected, and concerned. Like a hotline voice.

"I have more questions than you do," I assured her.

She seemed fine with that, but she didn't want to do it here. The place wasn't that crowded, but, like all the other pretty girls in the world, her sudden appearance had drawn its share of attention, and she didn't want to discuss her dead sister over entomatadas.

"I'd like to go to the lighthouse," I suggested.

Whenever possible, I prefer to talk to people about murder in environments related to the murder. It made them focus, and it made them nervous, but she didn't seem to mind at all.

"When you finish your cholesterol?"

It was hard not to smile. Helen Pavese had called her one of the "nerd" sisters, and maybe she was, but she was also a Jersey girl, and still a bit of a wiseass. She was also in the health racket, so maybe she was concerned about my health.

I paid the bill, and we drove my ETS to the extreme southern end of the Garden State. We parked close to the beautiful lighthouse (who doesn't like lighthouses?), where she informed me that it was the third one built on the spot, built in 1859, 157 feet high, 217 steps to the top.

I like her specificity, and I like the historical pride she took in her hometown. Maybe someday I'll tell her about Paterson and really impress the hell out of her. We walked over to the ocean, to one of the wooden Hawk Watch platforms, where the bird people come day after day to stare into the sky and look for peregrines and eagles, bald and golden, and where the local kids sometimes come late at night to do what kids do late at night.

But I didn't start with the dead sister, but rather with the guy who'd probably been killed for looking into her dead sister's murder ten years after the fact.

As the March sun began to dissipate, we sat down on a wooden bench and stared at the Atlantic. I'd been doing a lot of that in the past eighteen hours.

"What's with you and Colt?"

She shrugged.

"He liked me."

I'd assumed that. For one, who *wouldn't* like her, and, for two, they'd been out for dinner the night he was killed.

"Did you like him?"

"Yes."

She seemed willing to tell me more, so I prodded her.

"Tell me."

"He was very nice."

"Yeah, that's *exactly* what every guy likes to hear: 'You're very nice.'"

"But he was," she insisted. "He was polite, and thoughtful, and pleasant to be around."

"But—?"

"But he seemed rather sad. Damaged somehow."

"His past?"

"I really don't know. He said he grew up in Harrisburg, but then he lived in Mexico for a while, and his wife died down there."

"Any specifics?"

"None, and I didn't press him. The truth is, I really didn't know him that well, and I didn't want to ask him questions about the sadness in his life."

I understood, but, in my racket, it's *always* about the sadness in people's lives.

"There's something else," she said.

I waited.

"He proposed to me."

I was amazed, and I don't amaze easily. I guess Eddie was a fast worker.

"When?"

"At Tisha's."

"The night he died?"

"Yes."

"I thought you didn't know the guy?"

"I didn't. I hardly knew him at all. I met him once at my father's house after he'd agreed to take Nikki's case, and we went out to dinner three times. That was it."

She seemed astonished.

"He never even kissed me. He never even tried."

Which was hard to believe.

"The guy was a fool."

She let it slide, and I wondered why I'd said it. What was the matter with me?

"What did you say?"

"What do you think I said? I was very nice about it, and I said things like, 'but we hardly know each other' and 'let's wait and see what happens'—that kind of stuff. But, to be honest, I was rather spooked by it."

"How did he respond?"

"Like a perfect gentleman. Very polite, very understanding. He seemed more sad than hurt."

The guy was definitely way too "sad" to be a Colt.

I moved on.

"What about his mother's funeral?"

She shrugged again. There was something unintentionally and inexplicably sexual about her shrug. At least, I *assumed* it was unintentional.

"He left town for a few day, and told me his mother had died."

"Any specifics?"

"Nothing. I assumed he went to Harrisburg."

"You believed him?"

"Of course, I did. Why shouldn't I? When he got back to town he was wearing a little black band on his arm."

Rikki got suspicious.

Not of him. Of me.

"You don't *believe* people, do you?"

She sounded like a ten-year-old.

"Of course, I don't. Everyone I've ever met lies. Except for me."

"That's a lie right there."

"I suppose it is."

I changed the subject.

"Tell me about your ex."

"Whoa! Am *I* a suspect?"

"Of course, you are. Everyone on the planet's a suspect. Except for me."

"You've got trust issues, John Colt."

"Yeah, I've got lots of trust issues. Now tell me about your ex."

She did. He was a local realtor, whom she'd EMT-ed after he smacked up his pickup on Lafayette Street about a year ago. They married two months later, ("I must have been out of my mind"), and she regretted it from the two "I dos."

"I left him after two months. I was unhappy, and he seemed impervious, and I went back to live with my father. All of us do something stupid in our lives, and that's mine. It was doomed from the moment I patched up his facial lacerations and started to feel sorry for him."

"Why?"

She shrugged again, and I wondered how I could get her to do it again.

"He was loner, an only-child type. He went through the motions at work and barely got by. His big thing was deep-sea fishing, every weekend, and sitting on the couch and watching Eagles games. I'm a Giants fan."

"You seem to specialize in sad sacks."

"Yeah, but I'm trying to break the habit."

"Did he go gently into that good night?"

"At first, he didn't make a fuss. He signed the divorce papers when I asked him to, although he wasn't too happy about it."

"He still wants you back?"

"Yeah."

She felt it was time to defend herself. Which was hardly necessary.

"Some men find me attractive."

"Put me on the list."

She laughed at my idiocy, but I was appalled by it, so I pressed forward.

I knew there was more.

"Tell me the rest."

"It's embarrassing."

"Tell me."

"Ask my father."

"I'm asking you."

She shrugged again.

"He started stalking me."

"How?"

"Around town, on the web, stopping by the house. At first it was just annoying, but then he started with the threats."

"Like what?"

"Like 'You better come back,' and 'No one else is going to have you,' that kind of stuff."

"Did he ever get physical?"

"He grabbed me one night, and my father got a restraining order."

"Is he capable of violence?"

"I don't know."

"Does he have a record?"

"I don't know."

"Are you afraid of him?"

She hesitated, then she told me the truth.

"Yes."

I was wearing her out, and wearing the subject out, so I moved on.

To the dead sister.

"Did you guys ever switch identities?"

"Of course we did. Even the Bobbsey Twins had a mischievous streak."

"I read a few of those books when I was a kid. I liked the ones where they solved a mystery."

I guess I was ingratiating myself. I wondered if it was too obvious.

"Nikki and I read all seventy-two of them."

I liked her upmanship.

She thought it over.

(Meaning my "switching" question.)

"I guess you're thinking I might *really* be Nikki?"

"Why not? Stranger things have happened."

She laughed.

"I guess I *really* am a suspect."

"Everyone's a suspect."

"Except you."

The pretty bobbed-haired wiseass smiled mischievously, but I still needed more answers.

"What were you doing the night that your sister was sitting here with the other kids?"

"I was home by then. I'd had an EMT training class, and I came home afterwards, did a bit of homework, and then some reading."

"What?"

"*Persuasion.*"

"Great book."

It often surprises people that I've read a book, *any* book, but she took it right in stride. In her world, even a Paterson tough guy could get off on Jane Austen.

"Tell me about the car."

"The Mustang?"

"Yeah, the yellow Mustang."

"Daddy bought it for us when we turned sweet sixteen. Back then, ten years ago, we were still on our driver's permits."

"Where was it that night?"

"It was in the driveway, but it was gone when I got up the next morning. I figured that Nikki and Ronnie had taken it. Ronnie had a *real* driver's license."

"Was it full of gas?"

"Always. Since we shared the car, Daddy made us promise to fill it up every time before we brought it home. If it was in the driveway, it was full."

Which seemed peculiar to her.

"Is it important?"

"Maybe not."

She didn't bother to press it.

"Would you take me to the jetty?"

Which meant: would you take me to the place where they pulled your "screaming yellow" Mustang out of the ocean and found your identical twin sister dead inside the trunk?

"All right."

"You sure you're OK with it?"

Maybe I was showing too much concern.

"I'm fine. It was ten years ago."

We stood up.

"One more thing."

She waited, staring at the ocean.

"Who do *you* think did it?"

She didn't hesitate.

"Probably Izzy."

She didn't seem bitter, and she didn't seem vindictive. She was very matter of fact.

"Why?"

She thought about how she could explain herself.

"Izzy was always a bit odd, rough around the edges. You know what I mean? And she didn't have an alibi."

"That's it?"

"That's it. Maybe I'm wrong."

When I didn't say anything, she did.

"I hope so."

13

The Cove

WHAT'S ON YOUR MIND?"

We were sitting, reasonably comfortably, on the blackish rocks of the Cove Beach jetty. Cove Beach was the southernmost end of the Cape May beaches, close to Sunset Pavilion at Second Avenue. The Atlantic, black and impenetrable, was splashing around us, but never actually *on* us, and not too loud.

Almost gentle.

Softly in, softly out.

Cove Beach, as Rikki explained earlier, was extremely popular in the summer, generally laid back, and the best spot on the Cape for surfing.

Tonight, it was nothing but lonely, empty, and dark.

This was where they'd pulled the yellow Mustang from the ocean ten years ago, opened the trunk, and found pretty young Nikki inside, already dead, and, according to the coroner, drowned. With a sizable gash on the back of her head. Probably smashed with a rock. Which probably knocked her out before she was dumped in the trunk.

But, at the moment, it wasn't on my mind.

I'd been out here for at least an hour (or was it two?) with the dead girl's pretty sister (make that "beautiful"), talking all kinds of stuff and staring at the ocean. Talking about her EMT job, critical care, her twin sister, her failed marriage, her father, and the ocean she loved.

She told me about growing up with her father and her sister, about how "wonderful" (her word) her father was to the both of them, and how, in spite of everything, she missed having a mother.

Something I knew something about.

"No matter how good things are," she admitted, "a little girl without a mother is always a Little Girl Lost."

I get that.

Besides, I'm a very good listener, which is extremely important in my racket, but it wasn't just a job thing. I *liked* to listen; I liked to hear people talk about themselves. I even, I guess I'd have to admit, like people, even though most of them are self-centered morons.

Not this one.

Yeah, she was a Jersey girl, but Jersey girl *lite*. She had the attitude, but not the bitchiness. She was fun-loving, not reckless; outgoing, not loud; funny, not crude; blunt, not mean; confident, not supercilious.

She was also lovely.

What did the boss sing in that famous Waits song?

> *Cause nothing matters in this whole wide world*
> *When you're in love with a Jersey girl.*

Now the Jersey girl wanted to know what was on *my* mind.
I wasn't sure.

We'd gotten so comfortable with each other that there'd been long, numerous, and contented silences, as we'd stare out at the ocean she loved and think about whatever we wanted to think about.

When she asked me, I realized that I was thinking about something that had happened many years ago when I was just a boy. Something that had happened at the Jersey Shore. Something that I'd never told anyone about, not even my uncle. Not because it was embarrassing, but because I knew that I could never explain it properly. But, the truth is, you can never really explain *anything* in life properly.

So I told her.

Or tried to.

Why not?

I was fourteen. I was down at Seaside Heights, and I went into the water, and I saw this little girl. At that particular time in my life, I had three significant all-consuming interests in life: football, baseball, and murder. Girls, as a general category, wouldn't have made the top hundred.

But this one changed things.

All I could see was her pretty face, soaked with the ocean, with big wet eyes and completely drenched pixie light-brown hair. She was staring at me, so I stared back.

"What are you looking at?"

I hadn't been to charm school yet.

She wasn't intimidated in the least.

"Not much."

(Meaning me.)

But we both knew that *something* was up. There was a kind of inexplicable mutuality, some kind of affinity, some kind of unanticipated communion—as the ins-and-outs of the ocean waves and the subtle New Jersey currents, moved us, ever so gently back and forth, but never apart.

Then closer.

I could see that she was wearing a nothing-much yellow two-piece, with the top part not supporting very much. I moved myself behind her and gently put my arms around her. She didn't resist. She was still a little girl, thin, perfect, lovely, and I connected my hands in front of her stomach, careful not to touch any of her still maturing private parts.

I kissed her neck.

She didn't resist.

"Why did you do that?"

She seemed as baffled as me.

"I have no idea."

That was the best I could do.

"Maybe I should tell my sister's boyfriend."

"Who's he?"

"A cop."

"Not your father?"

"Nah, he's worthless."

Which broke my heart, which made me glad that I had her within my arms, protecting her.

"Did you like it?" I asked.

(Meaning the kiss.)

"Yes."

"Did *you* like it?" she asked.

"Yes."

My uncle had raised me to tell the truth.

I got *too* truthful:

"You're very beautiful," I said, realizing, for the first time in my life, that I was some kind of "romantic." Like all those dorks in the rom-com movies.

She seemed to like the idea.

"Do it again."

I didn't know if she wanted me to say it again or kiss her again, so I took my choice.

I kissed her neck. Then I moved around in front of her and kissed her wet and salty lips.

You know the "moment," right? When everything changes. When there's no turning back.

I held her for about an hour or so, and we talked and we didn't, and we asked each other lots of questions. She was a Jersey girl from Cherryville, down the shore with her older sister and her fiancé, a Bridgewater cop. We had no idea what we were doing, of course, but we wanted to meet again that night on the boardwalk if she could sneak away from her sister.

But she couldn't.

I followed her and her sister and her sister's cop all over the boardwalk that night, frustrated, of course, as we shot each other furtive "meaningful" glances, even though we had no idea what "meaningful" meant.

Then they left.

All I had left was an indelible image of her eating that giant whirl of pink cotton candy, and wishing that I could kiss the pink sugar off her oddly reddish lips. She wore yellow short-shorts, a "Giants" navy t-shirt over an unseen bra that had no real function, with a little yellow ribbon in her hair, and cute yellow Keds.

Why are women so lovely?

So irresistible?

"Was that the end of it?" Rikki wondered, wondering if I ever saw her again.

"The next day, I went back to the same spot where we'd met the day before, hoping that she'd be there, *knowing* that she'd be there, and she was. So were the guards, the cops, the paramedics, and the yellow tape that cordoned off our section of the beach. Her heart-crushed and debilitated sister was standing in the hot sand, held by her fiancé, both in disbelief. When they carried her sister's covered body to the ambulance, I watched it like you watch a movie. It wasn't real. I wasn't accustomed to death yet.

But that was the beginning.

"What happened?"

"A lifeguard told me she got caught in a riptide."

Rikki nodded.

Beach girls know about riptides.

"Later that night, I sat on the beach and stared at the ocean. I wasn't sad, but I was shocked and confused. I was also angry. *Very* angry. But I was impotent. I wanted to do something, I wanted to hurt someone, I wanted to arrest someone, but I couldn't arrest the Atlantic Ocean. Or God. Or life. Or anything else. But I *could* grow up like my uncle and arrest bastards and sons of bitches."

"Which you do."

"Which I do."

There was another one of our lovely silences.

Eventually, she spoke again:

"I want you to find my sister's killer."

"I will."

I was that simple.

When I drove her home, there was something I didn't like in the rear view mirror. When I stopped on Ocean Avenue, she got out and went inside her old man's house, a big and beautiful Victorian. I drove around the block, parked, and headed back to the front door. As I approached the entrance, an outdoor light came on, and there was a dark figure standing on the front porch. He had a weapon in his right hand, and the front door began to open.

It was Rikki.

"Don't move!" I called out, but he ignored me, so I pulled my Colt.

As Rikki opened the door, I tried again, as I rushed towards the house.

"Drop it!"

He lifted his weapon. Too bad for him.

I hope it doesn't sound vain, but I'm a dead shot with a handgun, especially a Python, the most accurate handgun in the world.

When I pumped a hole through his right thigh, he staggered a bit. Then he turned around to face me and raised his weapon.

I really don't like killing people, but when they're trying to kill me, I'm perfectly willing to make an exception.

I blew a tunnel through his brain, and he collapsed to the wooden floor of the porch.

Rikki looked down at the guy she'd married nine months ago.

"Eric?"

14

Benton Avenue

Thursday, March 26th
38°

I WAS LOOKING DOWNWARD, into Colt's swimming pool.

Fortunately, I don't need much sleep.

After the cops arrived, I spent a few hours at the Cape May PD, explaining why I'd killed one of their local citizens. Dawson showed up, and the boys and girls in blue treated me well. If I'd been a cop myself, I would have been buried under days and days of red tape, but as an ordinary citizen, albeit one with a PI's license and a license to carry, it was pretty routine. Especially since Anderson had a Ruger LC9 in his hand, had been stalking his ex-wife for months, had threatened her on numerous occasions, and still had an outstanding restraining order.

When the cops were done, I drove over to Colt's house on Benton Avenue, the scene of the murder. *His* murder. Dawson had given me the keys so I could look the place over. Just like his office, Colt's house was pretty Spartan, with very little in the way of decoration. Actually, not much in the way of anything. Dawson was right. The guy was a bit of a ghost.

Standing at the edge of the swimming pool, I mentally reconstructed the crime. The guy proposes to Rikki, gets the big "no," comes back home, has a drink, drops his clothes, and pops into his heated swimming pool. Then he swishes around for a while, probably thinking about Rikki (which would be impossible *not* to think about after spending the evening with her), then gets out of the pool and gets himself shot, pretty much point blank, in the forehead.

Ballistics says it was likely a Beretta, definitely not Eric Anderson's Ruger LC9.

But Edward Colt wasn't just killed, he was assassinated. There was no hesitation. Maybe even no rage. It was like a hit. Cold and clean.

Which was *nothing* like whatever had happened to Nikki O'Brien ten years ago.

I sat down on one of the pool chairs and read over Nonna's "Rikki" report. She must have sent it while I was on the beach with the subject of the report, telling her about something I'd never told anyone else before.

Everything except the girl's name.

Which was Sandy.

> *Rikki O'Brien (age 26, EMT nurse):*
>
>   *Rikki and her sister and her father were abandoned by the twins' mother (Kitty Walsh O'Brien) soon after the birth. The judge seems to have done an excellent job raising his pretty twin daughters, who were, apparently, inseparable, always dressed in cute, matching, classic outfits and dresses. The girls were stunningly attractive. (I'm sure you've seen the pictures.) They also, as far as I can tell, had virtually identical personalities.*
>
>   *They did a bit of modeling when they were little girls, but they were much more interested in grades, friends, and sports.*

They were very popular "good girl" types, goodie-goodies, known as the "Bobbsey Twins" (even though, as every idiot knows, the two pairs of twins in the Bobbsey Twins books were fraternal boy-girl twins, which I'm sure you know, Mr. Colt), who were copresidents of their sophomore and junior classes. They also played the two forward positions on the girls' basketball team, edited the yearbook, did charity work, etc., ad nauseam. Not to mention straight A's. They we're also, as seems perfectly logical, beach girls and strong swimmers.

Nothing illegal.

Apparently no drugs.

The do-gooder twins naturally wanted to "help people," so they planned to go to Rutgers together and become nurses, which was why they were doing EMT training in high school.

After the murder, Rikki seems to have had a rough time, staying at home for a year and finishing high school online. Then she got up off her ass and got her nursing degree at Rutgers, worked the emergency room at Cape Regional Medical Center, and then decided that she preferred working EMT, where she met her ex, Eric Anderson, when he crashed his car. They lasted two months, and she went back home to daddy. When Anderson started bugging her, they got a restraining order.

I like her, Jack. A lot. Maybe if she's not a murderer, you should marry her.

Love, Nonna

Earlier, when I'd killed her husband, she looked up from the dead corpse on her front porch and looked into my eyes, wondering: "Are you all right, Jack?"

15

The Killing

Thursday, March 26th
36°

THE DESPERATE FATHER is searching for his missing daughter.

As he talks to his wife on the phone, he drives his truck to Discovery Park where his daughter's pink sweater has been found. He sees the cops and salvage workers standing near a drenched car that they've just hoisted from the lake.

Behind the car, the senior homicide detective, Sarah Linden, tells the other cops to open the trunk.

When the father pulls up at the perimeter, he immediately gets out of his truck and goes up to the cops guarding the scene.

"What's going on?"

His voice is fearful, and his terrified wife can hear him over the phone.

At the rear of the car, Detective Linden sees the dead body of Rosie Larsen, still submerged in the water in the trunk.

At the perimeter, the cops have to restrain the struggling father, who seems to understand what's happening.

He calls out for his child.

"Rosie!"

Linden walks up to the father.

"You can't be here, Mr. Larsen."

"Is it my daughter?"

He's desperate. When she doesn't respond, he repeats himself.

"Is it my daughter?!"

She can't tell him.

"I'm sorry. You can't be here."

Linden walks back to the car, as the cops continue to restrain the struggling father.

He screams.

"Rosie!"

His wife, gradually comprehending what's happening, sobs uncontrollably.

The father calls out again:

"That's my baby girl!"

Linden, back at the car, looks at the dead body, no longer submerged. She stares, in a close-up, at the bindings on the girl's hands and feet, her drowned face, and the little butterfly necklace around the girl's throat.

Rosie's necklace.

I was now back at Congress Hall, sitting in my room, watching the end of the pilot episode of *The Killing* on my laptop. I saw it years ago, when it first came out. It was exceptionally well written, well directed, and well acted, most powerfully by the lead, Mireille Enos as Sarah Linden.

The show's tag was, "Who Killed Rosie Larsen?"

That was Linden's problem. Mine was, "Who killed Nikki O'Brien?"

Yesterday, when Nikki's father walked into my office and jarred my memory about the cold case, I wondered if there might be some possible connection with the television show.

Did the Nikki O'Brien killer imitate *The Killing*?

Impossible.

The show premiered in April 2011, six years after Nikki's murder.

Did the TV series imitate the O'Brien killing?

Highly unlikely. It was based on a Danish television series from 2007, which, apparently, didn't include a trunk murder.

Regardless, it was impossible *not* to think about the Cape May murder as "*The Killing* Killing," a term that Dawson had used at the Lobster House.

Enough.

I was getting punchy, maybe stupid.

Maybe it was time to shut my eyes for a bit.

Then Dawson texted.

> *When EC left town, his phone pinged in Kinnelon, New Jersey. Ever hear of it?*

Of course, I've heard of it. Kinnelon is up in my neck of the woods, not that far from Paterson. Which means that Edward Colt lied about going to Harrisburg, Pennsylvania, and he probably also lied about going to his mother's funeral.

Since my cell was already out, I checked Roxs's text-for-the-day, then reread her text from a month ago.

> *I'm standing at 51 W. 1st Street, Riverside, Iowa, the future birthplace of Captain James T. Kirk, March 22, 2228.*

I smiled and shut the thing off.

II

New Jersey invented fun: beaches, lakes, rivers, mountains, resorts, casinos, racetracks, even a rodeo, not to mention the greatest amusement park in the world: New York City.

— Thomas C. Colt

16

Shoreline Lanes

I 'VE GOT NOTHING to say."

    I was afraid of that.

Actually, it was Mitchell Cain who should have been "afraid of that."

I was standing at the counter of the dimly lit, mostly empty Shoreline Lanes. Off in the distance, a few of the alleys were active, with an intermittent smashing of pins, but I wasn't paying attention. I was staring at the manager, a worthless endomorph in a food-stained Raiders t-shirt.

I hate the Raiders.

I took off my tie, wrapped it around his neck, and watched his eyes start to bulge with the pressure.

It was an improvisation.

I'd never done it before, but I liked it. Yeah, the tie was a Kooples, a somewhat expensive Kooples, but I had almost fifty more in my closet at home in Paterson. Besides, it was well crafted, well made, and would probably come away from its unexpected diversion relatively undamaged.

Suddenly, a cute little girl in a pretty blue dress, maybe eight years old, appeared at the counter, wanting to drop off her shoes.

"Is he all right?" she asked, which I thought was a pretty stupid question, even for an eight-year-old.

"He was rude to me," I explained.

She thought it over, then fully accepted my explanation. Who likes rudeness? Right? She walked away, letting her little mind float back to whatever little girls think about.

As for Cain, he started gagging a bit, which I found unnecessary, rather disgusting, and a bit showy. Then he started bobbing his head up and down, desperately, as if he'd reconsidered and was now more than eager to talk. Being a reasonable man, I loosened my tie and put it back where it belonged, beneath the collar of my Brooks Brothers shirt, oddly complimenting my black Armani suit.

Today was "suspect day," and I was starting things off with the eyewitness who had seen the yellow Mustang gliding over the beach before vanishing into the water near the Cove Beach jetty.

When the moron finally collected himself, he was definitely ready to talk. Actually, he was ready to do pretty much *anything* I wanted. The earlier lack of cooperation with its hyper-confident "nobody messes with me" belligerence was a thing of the past, almost as if it had never existed. I nodded at the far corner of the alley's café, and we went over and sat down at a small table.

He said nothing, obviously concerned about setting me off again, so I initiated the grand inquisition.

"Tell me."

He didn't say, "But I already told the cops a million times back then," or "I told that other investigator last week," he *told* me.

"I was walking my dog—"

"What kind?"

He seemed surprised.

"Stabler's a Doberman."

You can tell a lot about a person, sometimes too much, by the kind of dog he or she owns.

Not to mention its name.

I waited for more.

"It was late, very late, almost 4:00 in the morning, and I was walking Stabler along the promenade next to the beach. The truth is, I don't sleep that well."

"Boohoo, moron."

Yeah, I know, that sounds really stupid, but I've learned over the years that bozos like Cain get really creeped out when someone like me—big, intimidating, and potentially violent—makes fun of them like a child. It's very unnerving, and Cain was unnerved. He glanced at my shades, glanced at my tie, looked away, and continued his narrative.

"I was approaching the south end of the beach, when I saw, in the moonlight, a yellow Mustang gliding over the sand towards the ocean. I was astonished. I couldn't believe what I was seeing. It was like a dream, and I stopped in my tracks. So did Stabler. Only later did I remember about the reclamation."

No standard-issue vehicle could "glide" over the sand, not even in early April when the sand is cold and harder. The reason that Nikki's yellow Mustang glided over the sand was because it wasn't moving on the sand. It was driving over a temporary mat-road that the Army Corps guys had laid down for access to the jetty.

Back in 2003, Hurricane Isabel had battered both the Outer Banks in North Carolina and Hampton Roads in Virginia. When it moved north, it created a state of emergency in five different states—Pennsylvania, Maryland, West Virginia, New Jersey, and

Delaware—killing fifty-six along the way. In Wildwood, nine miles north of Cape May, a surfer was killed, and the blast of the winds and the ocean surges severely eroded the Cape May beaches and pounded the Cove Beach jetty. Two years later, the town managed to get a grant from the feds to help pay for the restitution of the jetty, and several of the remaining armor stones were replaced and supplemental core stones were added.

The project initiated at the beginning of April, the month that Nikki was murdered.

"Then I dialed 911."

"Who was driving the car?"

"I couldn't tell. It was too far away."

As Helen Pavese, the lead detective back then, had told me on her front porch yesterday afternoon, "Either someone rigged the gas pedal somehow—although we never found any signs of tampering—or someone got out of the car in the ocean and made it to shore behind the jetty. Which is why the dope with the dog never saw the driver."

I looked at the dope with the dog.

"You saw the kids the previous day. In the early evening."

"Yeah, they came in and bowled a few games."

"I don't like coincidences."

Meaning that I didn't like the fact that he'd seen them here at the bowling alley and then seen the Mustang thirty-three hours later.

"Sometimes a coincidence is just a coincidence, right?"

Yeah, he was right, but I wasn't about to agree with him.

"Tell me about Thursday night."

He shrugged.

"They seemed like nice kids. Having a good time. I wasn't paying much attention."

"How many?"

"Four girls and two boys."

I looked at him, fixedly, intently, the way a peregrine looks at a rabbit before the descent.

"I'm sure there's more, Cain. I *know* there's more."

I was bluffing, of course.

He squirmed a bit.

"Some woman showed up and talked to one of the girls for a few minutes."

"Describe her."

"Pretty, youngish, maybe early thirties. Dressed country. Sloppy. She had a Piney look about her."

"Did you hear anything?"

"No. Nothing."

"Why didn't you tell the cops ten years ago?"

"I forgot about it."

I let him stare at the black sheen off the lenses of my Ray-Bans. Then he looked down at my tie again and elaborated.

"That's *exactly* what happened. When I remembered it later, I decided that I was already too involved, so I never said anything to that woman cop. She thought I was a suspect."

"So do I."

Which made him nervous.

So I made him even more nervous.

"If I find out that you're holding anything back, I'll toss your fat ass in jail and cut Stabler's head off."

"Look, I promise, there's *nothing* more."

The guy's promise was as worthless as he was.

I looked at him hard.

"Go away and rent some shoes."

17

Gingerbread House

Friday, March 27th
45°

W E WERE FULL that night."

"Let me see."

The kid working the desk turned the screen in my direction, and I quickly checked the names on the B&B's register for April 8, ten years ago, the night of Nikki's "lost" day.

Nothing of interest.

"Thanks, kid."

He smiled a friendly smile that wasn't just a "work" smile. He was probably a local kid who actually enjoyed working at the Gingerbread House.

Why not?

I went outside on Gurney Street, a block from the ocean. Why shouldn't a young kid be content to live and work in a town like Cape May? I don't often use the words "lovely" and "pretty" for anything but the female of the species, but Cape May was an undeniably lovely and pretty town.

I might even risk "enchanting."

With its tree-lined streets.

Its beaches.

Its assemblage of beautiful Victorian houses that looked like the workshop of some giant dollhouse maker.

With gingerbread lace, stained-glass windows, fretwork, feather boarding, cupolas, captain's walks, porches, verandahs, and storybook gardens.

The Gingerbread House, Nikki and Rikki's favorite, was no exception, built in 1869 and designed by Stephen Decatur Button, who'd designed over forty of the town's oversized dollhouses.

I went from one to another to another. . . .

It was a pleasant afternoon, and everyone was exceedingly helpful, especially when I told them that I'd been hired by Judge O'Brien and that I was looking into his daughter's murder, which might have happened ten years ago, but which no one in this town had ever forgotten.

After checking out the John Wesley Inn, right next door, I turned left on Columbia Avenue, which was really more of a "street." Then I turned left on Ocean Street and checked out the Humphrey Hughes House and the Columbia House.

Nothing.

I'm not much of a techie, although it helps a lot in my line of work, but one extremely useful thing about the web is the fact that so many businesses still have easy access to their business records, even from ten years ago.

Then I tried Queen Victoria, one of the most famous B&B's in Cape May, located at 102 Ocean Street, with a pleasingly odd color, some kind of light blue-green-gray, and an orange roof.

A well-kept, helpful woman in her fifties, showed me the screen and the registry. Just like the Gingerbread, they were full that night, and as I scanned the names, I spotted what I was looking for:

William Kelly

He'd paid in cash, and he'd signed his hometown as:

Georgetown, Delaware!

With an exclamation mark.

I thanked the lady, went outside, and called my gal Friday.

"Colt's badass detective agency."

I had no idea that she was answering the phone like that, but I didn't mind.

"I'm looking for Luca Salerno's ugly grandmother."

"You've got the wrong number. His *ugly* grandmother lives in Elmwood Park, a pretentious euphemism for East Paterson."

I paid no attention.

"Tell her that her boss wants her to check out the name 'William Kelly' from ten years ago. Check him in Jersey, Maryland, Delaware, and Johns Hopkins."

"I don't have a boss."

I hung up.

Whenever you talked to Luca's Nonna, you always had the feeling that you'd gotten the worse of the exchange.

18

The Cape May-Lewes Ferry

I'M NOT MUCH for boats.

I'm not really afraid of them, they just give me the creeps. I'm not afraid of snakes either, but they also give me the creeps.

I guess I'm a land-animal.

I was sitting at a little table on the upper third-deck of MV *New Jersey*, one of three huge ferries that crisscrossed the Delaware Bay from Cape May to Lewes, Delaware. Seventeen miles over and seventeen miles back. It was a pleasant March afternoon, with maybe a bit too much sun, so I was glad, as always, that I was wearing my polarized shades.

I was thinking about what Samuel Johnson, who was one of my all-time favorites, once said:

> *Being in a ship is like being in jail, with the chance of being drowned.*

She walked on the deck and wiped away my negatives.

Ronnie Miller was now twenty-eight years old, but she was looking closer to eighteen. Back in the year of the murder, she was Nikki and Rikki's closest friend. An all-American beach-type, trim, tanned, and very pretty. Something along the lines of a Jennifer Lawrence, but her hair was a pretty red, affirmatively red.

She walked over to my table wearing a cute little sailor's uniform, and I stood up before we sat down.

She smiled a redhead's smile.

"Ask me anything, tough guy."

I liked her. Who wouldn't?

At least with suspect number two, I wouldn't have to take off my tie.

I started easily, with a few throwaway questions, and she answered them just as easily. She admitted that she wasn't much of student back then, or ever, and had never bothered with college. Her father was the captain of the boat we were sitting on, the MV *New Jersey*, and she'd been working with him ever since she was in high school.

"I'm all for nepotism," she assured me.

She smiled easily. She was easy to be with. One might even use the silly word "fun."

Eventually, I got to the boys.

"Did Sonny take an interest in you?"

"Not really."

"What was he like?"

"Sweet, kind of goofy, looking forward to getting back home."

"Which was where?"

"Some place in North Jersey."

"Did he show any interest in either Rita or Izzy?"

"Not that I noticed."

"I wonder why?"

She shrugged.

"Was he jealous of Billy?"

"I never saw any of that. They seemed like real close pals. Typical boys."

"What did Billy look like?"

"Exactly what any young girl would like to look at. I'd guess he was about five ten, lean and perfect, with soft brown hair and soft brown eyes. He wore black jeans, deck shoes, and a red windbreaker like the one James Dean wore in *Rebel Without a Cause*. He was very easy to look at."

"So are you."

She smiled. She seemed to enjoy the impertinence.

"Why aren't you married?"

Sure, it was rude, but she didn't seem to mind. She looked down at her ringless finger.

"I was for a bit. I lasted a few more months than Rikki did."

She was very good-natured, even about her personal tragedies.

"Why don't you try it again?"

She shrugged.

"You know the Pam Tillis song, 'All the Good Ones are Gone'?"

"Yeah."

I *did* know the song, something about a thirty-four-year-old woman, who's out with her gal pals for a few margaritas, and she thinks about guys, and flirting, and getting "hit on," and she decides that there's no "good ones" left.

"Maybe *that's* why," she decided.

I was glad I wasn't a woman in today's world.

"Do you still see Rikki?"

"Of course, we meet every Thursday at the Mad Batter. Like the girls in the song."

I wondered if I was starting to fall for her, which was perfectly ridiculous, so I changed the subject.

"Did you ever talk to Edward Colt?"

"No. We were supposed to meet on Wednesday, the day after he was killed."

"Did the twins have any favorite teachers back in high school?"

"Sure, we were *all* in love with Mr. Sykes. The biology teacher."

"Did he take a special interest in the twins?"

"I guess you could say that, but there was nothing weird about it. *Everyone* liked the twins."

"Was there anyone who *didn't* like the twins?"

"Not really."

Then she remembered.

"Actually, Mrs. Rockingham never really liked the girls."

"Rita's mother?"

"Yeah."

"Why?"

"I don't know. Maybe she was jealous. They were always competing with Rita."

"And beating her?"

"And beating her. But Rita never seemed upset about it. I understand she's now a lawyer and doing nicely."

"What about Izzy?"

"She worked in a bunch of hair salons then vanished. I don't know where she is. Nobody does."

An obnoxious boat horn blasted obnoxiously, probably meaning that I better get my ass off the damned floating contraption or I'd end up in the state of Delaware.

When I stood up, she sat right where she was, maybe thinking about ten years ago, when she was a happy young girl with happy young friends until the recondite hideousness of life intruded itself into their lives and one of them got herself murdered.

Ronnie looked up at me, and I felt the hurt of her sadness.

"I think about her every single day."

19

Field of Dreams

I WALKED INTO its comforting greenness. The perfect and trim greenness of the outfield. An American baseball field. One of the most beautiful places on earth.

What did Babe Ruth say?

Something like:

Baseball is the greatest game in the world.

It's hard to argue. It's especially hard to argue with a guy like Babe Ruth, even for someone who lived and breathed football his entire youth, even though I got pretty serious about center field every year when the new spring arrived.

Now I was standing, once again, in center field, thinking about Willie Mays, Mickey Mantle, and Mike Trout. The young boys of spring were warming up over in left field, tossing the hardball around, kidding with each other, enjoying the magic of their late teens at the Lower Cape May Regional High School.

Which is quite a mouthful.

The head coach, dressed exactly like his kids in a Cape May Tigers uniform, with a black-and-blue cap, walked across the grass in my direction.

Ten years ago, Tommy Garrison was the "boyfriend." Now he was a history teacher at the exact same high school where he'd once planned to take Nikki O'Brien to the junior prom until she ended up dead in a car trunk. He was pleasant looking in an ordinary kind of way, an ordinary "jockish" kind of way, solid, maybe a few pounds heavier than when he was a big-shot high school athlete.

He walked right up and shook my hand. But I was wrong. There *was* something unique about him. His eyes were a very peculiar green, oddly matching the spring greenness of the surrounding outfield.

"Rikki said I should talk to you."

He was polite, doing his best to conceal his reluctance. I can't say that I blamed him. I wouldn't want to talk to me either.

I didn't see any reason to waste his time or mine.

"You never married?"

Like Ronnie, he was ringless.

He shrugged.

"I lost the one I loved."

The guy, for his age, was an athletic specimen, but he was also an ocean of sadness.

"What about her sister? Was there really any difference between them?"

I wanted to see if he had a temper, but he took my unpleasantness in stride.

"Enough."

"Tell me."

But he couldn't actually articulate it.

"No, I guess you're right, there wasn't much difference. But I fell for the one and not the other."

"Could you tell them apart?"

"No," he admitted. "Never."

If nothing else, the guy seemed honest.

"She was out with another guy that night," I said.

Meaning his girlfriend.

"So they say."

"And you didn't have much of an alibi."

"I guess not. It was the middle of the night, and I was home asleep. I was eighteen years old."

"How did you deal with it?"

"Not too well. I'm not ashamed to admit that Nikki's death destroyed my life. I wanted to do what Rikki did and hide myself away from the world, but I didn't. I pressed on. Like a zombie."

"And now?"

"I suppose I'm coming around. At least, that's what my mother says."

He looked over at his baseball boys.

"I've got the kids, and my classes, and baseball. Beautiful baseball."

"Would you like to kill whoever did it?"

He looked back at me directly. He was fine with the question.

"Definitely. Yes."

He remembered and admitted:

"I used to dream about it. And daydream about it. I still do sometimes."

"Who's in the dream?"

"It's pretty vague, but I know who it is."

"Who is it?"

"Some kid named Billy."

20

Campbell Funeral Home

Friday, March 27th
40°

I WALKED OVER to the coffin and looked down at the dead guy. He didn't look like a Colt to me. If he was some kind of relative, he must have been a whole bunch of "removes" away.

But I doubted it.

The Edward Colt viewing was winding down, and the place was eerily empty except for Rikki, her father, and some silent-as-the-grave funeral guy lurking in a far corner.

I went over and checked the guest list. Eight names in three hours. That's less than three an hour. Not much of a send-off into the great beyond, but, of course, the guy had only moved to Cape May a few months ago. None of the names, as far as I knew, were related to the Nikki case, and, aside from the two O'Brien's, the only one I recognized was Dawson, who was probably hoping against hope that he could somehow prove that Eric Anderson, in a fit of jealous rage, had killed the guy in the wooden box who'd been dating his ex-wife.

I wasn't buying it.

Rikki came over, dressed in black, in one of those "little black dresses," looking perfectly beautiful. I tried not to notice what was impossible *not* to notice.

"Thanks for letting me out of my cage."

She smiled.

After I killed her husband the other night, I told her old man not to let her out of the house.

"What about the wake?" he asked.

"All right."

"What about the funeral?"

"No way."

I thought I should say something about killing her husband.

"I'm sorry what happened happened."

She appreciated it.

Actually, I wasn't sorry at all, the bastard was about to blow my head off.

"You know," she confided, "I've been thinking a lot about Eric, and about Eric and me, and I realize that I really didn't know him at all."

"It happens."

She seemed baffled by the idea that you could marry someone, live with him (or her) for two months, and never really *know* them.

"It happens all the time," I assured her.

She shifted the subject.

"I think you saved my life."

"Could be. But I definitely saved mine."

"I bet you do it all the time."

"Yeah, every day of the week."

My cell pinged.

We ignored it.

I thought I should say something nice.

"You shouldn't wear that dress in here."

"Why not?"

She was genuinely confused.

"You might wake up the dead."

She looked at me.

Mischievously.

"You're a very bad boy."

"Thank you."

"When do I get released back into the world?"

"Let's talk about it later tonight."

"Fine."

I nodded at her old man, left the room, and found another unlit room. This one was stiffless, not that I cared. Then I checked out the latest report from the Insult-Grandma:

> *Thomas Garrison (age 27, high school teacher):*
>
> *Tommy was Nikki's boyfriend, which I'm sure you've figured out by now. He'd known the twins since grammar school, and he and Nikki started dating in their sophomore year. He was her first-and-only, and I think she was his first as well. He was quite the catch back then. Good-looking, popular, bright, from a well-adjusted family (dad: a local contractor; mom: a kindergarten teacher). He was also an all-county righty with a minor-league-level fastball, a decent curve, and a mean cutter. When Nikki was killed, he'd already had several college scholarship offers, including Rutgers, Lehigh, and Penn State.*
>
> *After graduation, he went to Lehigh but never played ball. I'm not sure why. But he coached the pitchers*

on the team and majored in history (American). These days he teaches at Cape May High, and his teacher ratings are through the roof. He's unmarried, and I'm sure all the little high school girls dream about him in bed at night.

I realize it's not much of a report, but I've already decided that he didn't commit the crime. He's too much of a "nice" boy, the kind we're incapable of procreating in North Jersey.

By the way, someone named Luca, who claims to be my progeny, said to "say hello to the beachboy," who must be you.

Love, Nonna

To clear my mind, I checked out Roxs's text-for-the-day, then reread her text from a month ago, realizing that I hadn't thought about her all day long:

I'm standing in the moonlit Mount Moriah Cemetery looking down at the tombstone of the holder of aces and eights.

She'd stopped in Deadwood.

Of course, she did.

I remembered sitting with my princess in White Castle one day, and we talked about Wild Bill, and how he loved his Colt Navy Models, with ivory grips and engraved silver plating, who was, inexplicably, carrying a Smith & Wesson when Jack McCall burst into Nuttal & Mann's Saloon on August 1, 1876, yelled, "Damn you! Take that!" and shot Wild Bill in the back, dead, with nothing but aces and eights in his "dead man's hand."

"I don't want you playing no poker," she decided.

"Fine."

21

Atlantic Cape

H OW OFTEN DID YOU DREAM about them naked?"

He was stunned.

Stunned in a way that only a pretentious college professor can be stunned. As if the detritus of a far distant world (the real world) had somehow invaded and contaminated his academic fantasyland.

I loved it.

I also loved being me. I know that sounds almost as self-absorbed as all the pretentious college professors of the world, but it's true.

When you're me, nobody looks at you and wonders if you're politically correct. If you're polite. If you're sensitive. On the contrary, they fully anticipate the contrary. They expect me (maybe even want me) to say whatever the hell I want to say, in whatever the hell way I want to say it, and they fully accept it. They tolerate it. They don't sweat it. They know that there's absolutely no way that the "problem" can be rectified. I'm like the bad little boy that everyone's given up on, and whenever little wiseass Johnny gets into trouble, they all shrug, or sigh, or say, "Oh, well, that's Johnny for you," or, "Oh, well, isn't little Johnny just impossible!" or, maybe just, "Oh, well," and then everyone presses on.

His Bio 101 class had just been dismissed, and the room was empty, except for the two of us. I was standing in front of his desk, and I had the distinct feeling that he was wishing that anyone else on the planet was standing in front of him.

Ten years ago, Aaron Sykes was the "cool" high school teacher, popular, energetic, and funny. He even made biology interesting, and all the kids loved him. Including Nikki, Rikki, Tommy, Ronnie, etc. Now he was looking like a forty-two-year-old loser adjunct at Atlantic Cape Community College in Mays Landing, forty-two miles north of Cape May, with a stupid-looking thick brown beard and nothing much on top.

Divorced and kidless.

"Never," he said, referring to my "naked" question.

He seemed thoughtful.

Maybe I was wrong. Maybe the guy really did have some substance. Maybe he was even capable of telling the truth.

"Explain it to me."

He thought about it. Back to ten years ago, when he had the world on a string.

"Did you ever do any teaching?" he wondered.

"Do I look like I've ever done any teaching?"

He thought that over, too.

"When you teach young kids—"

He clarified.

"When you teach young girls, you can't help certain natural attractions. No normal male could resist some kind of an attraction, some kind of allurement or endearment, to the likes of Nicole and Erica O'Brien. We all know that students have 'crushes' on their teachers, well, Mr. Colt, it works the other way too. But I wouldn't call it a 'crush' exactly."

"What would you call it?"

He shrugged.

"Something like: 'I wish I was ten years younger.'"

"Did you ever pretend that you were?"

"Never. Not with them, and not with anyone. But I'm not going to stand here and pretend that I wasn't fascinated by the both of them."

I looked at him hard.

"Why are you telling me this?"

"Why not? I've developed an affinity for the truth over the years. So why not tell you? Besides, I had absolutely *nothing* to do with whatever happened to Nikki. I wished nothing but the very best for both her and her sister."

"Was there anyone back then who *didn't* wish them the very best? Anyone you were suspicious of?"

"I always thought that there was something 'off' about their friend, Rita."

"Rockingham?"

"Yes."

"In what way?"

He shrugged again.

"I don't know. Maybe she had a crush on one of them. Maybe both of them. I don't know."

That was something I hadn't considered.

I asked a few more questions, then I shook the guy's hand. I was hopeful that his new relationship with the truth would be a lasting one.

When I found an empty classroom, I switched on the light and got right to the Nonna's new report. The one I was waiting for:

> *William "Billy" Kelly (murderer?):*
>
> *Here's what I've got so far:*
>
> *Billy grew up in Packanack Lake, Wayne, New Jersey, raised by his unmarried aunt, Rosaline Kelly. I'm not sure what happened to his parents. After grammar school (get this!), he went to DePaul (just like you and Luca) and played on the football team (running back). You guys missed him by a year. I guess he was a serious student since he got himself into Hopkins before he vanished ten years ago. His Aunt Rosaline is now dead.*
>
> *Tomorrow, I'll check with his teachers and get a hold of his DMV photo. Etc.*
>
> *This is getting intriguing, Jackie. Maybe I'll come down there with some sunblock and solve this thing, and you can sit here at my desk and look things up and answer the phone.*
>
> *Love, Nonna*

It *was* intriguing.

Who was this guy?

And where the hell was he?

22

Oceanview Lodge

I LIKE PHOTOGRAPHS.

Especially the kind you can hold in your hand.

Especially crime-scene photos and crime-related photos.

I was sitting on the couch in O'Brien's living room, looking at a handful of photos in the second category. Photos of his daughters, photos with their father, photos with their friends.

Mostly pictures of the Bobbseys.

In their twin bassinets, in their matching toddler outfits, in their Holy Communion whites and veils, in an wide assortment of studio model-shots from when they were around ten, each more lovely, more adorable, than the last.

Etc.

In a bunch of the other shots, Ronnie was with them, smiling as always, and I spotted both Rita and Izzy in a few of the others. All pretty young girls, all looking happy to be alive, at the Cape May beach, at the New Jersey shore.

There were also a few with Tommy, standing between the indistinguishable twins.

Innocent kids' stuff.

The father was sitting in a nearby chair, silent, waiting, watching, and his daughter was out in the kitchen talking on her cellphone to someone. Maybe Ronnie. The only words I overheard were "house arrest," and I shot her a glance, and she smiled back, mouthing two words that looked like, "the warden."

I looked at the judge.

"Could you tell them apart?"

It was a pretty stupid question to ask a father: can you tell your children apart? But I often ask people stupid questions. You never know where they'll lead.

"No," he said.

That was it. Just "No." It was just that simple, and I was very surprised. Since he'd already anticipated my next question, he decided to help me out.

"When they were babies, Rikki wore a little gold ankle bracelet engraved with her name, and Nikki wore a silver one. When they got older, I got them gold and silver bracelets for their wrists, and I asked them to never take them off."

"Did they?"

"I don't think so. Ask Rikki."

I placed the photos on the coffee table in front of me.

"I don't see any photos of Kitty Walsh."

"I tossed them all when she left. It was foolish, and stupidly impulsive, and I've regretted it. Especially when the girls would ask what their mother looked like."

"What *did* she look like?"

"A very pretty country girl, who crushed my heart the moment I saw her."

He caught himself. Richard O'Brien was a pleasant man, but

a reserved one. The kind of guy who didn't feel very comfortable revealing too much about himself.

I couldn't have cared less.

"Tell me about the 'moment.'"

He thought it over. Weighing his personal reservations, his personal proprieties.

"All right."

I waited.

"I guess it was rather ordinary, but it seemed unique and special to me."

I waited some more.

"I saw her on the Wildwood boardwalk one night. She was barefoot, wearing jeans and a red flannel shirt, and eating a strawberry ice cream cone. She looked like she was twelve, but she was seventeen. I stopped and stared at her, rather moronically, which is definitely not the kind of thing I'd usually do, and she looked back at me and she smiled and said, 'Who wears a suit on the boardwalk?' We were married two months later, she had the twins nine months later, and she left a week after the kids were born."

How does a man sum up the most important and consequential relationship in his life? Well, that's how Richard O'Brien just did it.

"That's it," he said, alerting me to the obvious fact that *that* was all that he wanted to remember.

"Do you give her money?"

He looked at me with interest, with curiosity.

"I find your rudeness very interesting."

"How's that?"

"Because it's somehow not as offensive as it should be."

"Maybe that's because you think I'm the only guy on the planet who can figure out who killed your daughter."

"Can you?"

"Yes."

He nodded, then he answered my rude question.

"Yes, I give her a stipend."

He didn't wait for me to ask how much.

"Five hundred dollars a month."

"Did she ask for it?"

"No."

"Did she ever ask for more?"

"No. As a matter of fact, I haven't spoken with her—or communicated with her—since she walked out that door."

He looked over at the front door, as if he could still see her cute Piney ass exiting his life forever.

Maybe I needed to change the subject.

"I'd like to see Nikki's room."

"It's Rikki's room."

"She moved in after the murder?"

"No, they always lived in the same room. Always. They never wanted separate rooms."

I guess I understood.

"We'll have to check with Rikki first," he said, respecting her privacy.

"I already did."

He believed me, so we stood up and went upstairs.

It was a handsome house, one of the oldest and largest on Ocean Avenue, right across from the north end of the Cape May beaches, not far from Helen Pavese's house. Maybe it's not fair to stereotype people, but we all do it, and I do it more than most. The place was exactly like what you'd expect from a respected judge of some local distinction. Traditional, comfortable, expensive in a completely unobtrusive way, and very livable. It was way too big for a man and his two twin daughters, let alone a man and his only daughter, but I had the feeling that it was always "homey" to all three of them.

The Rikki/Nikki room was smaller than I expected, with little twin beds with matching pink comforters, with "Nikki" written in pink on the left bed's headboard and "Rikki" written on the right one. Nearby, there were matching end tables and matching little wooden desks, one with an open laptop, and the other looking meticulously clean but unused and abandoned. Back then, the girls were sixteen, and there were still a few remnants of their teenage years in the room: several basketball trophies, high school pompoms, photos of Dwight Yoakam, Tim Duncan, and the Boss.

There was also some Rutgers stuff, along with two small, hand-carved religious statues, one on each desk (Saint Anthony for Rikki, Saint Monica for Nikki). On the walls, there were various framed photographs of lighthouses at night, all very striking, and I recognized Old Barney and the Cape May Lighthouse. On the wall between the two beds, there was a small framed picture of a turn-of-the-twentieth-century nurse.

Whom I recognized.

There was also a white, fresh-and-ready, EMT uniform laying out, very neatly, across Rikki's bed.

"She sleeps in Nikki's bed?" I wondered.

"I didn't know."

The father didn't seem surprised.

"I need to snoop around."

I looked in the two closets, read the book titles in the two bookcases, and started opening the drawers in Nikki's little desk.

In the bottom drawer, there was a Beretta 92.

I pulled out my handkerchief, secured the gun, and lay it carefully on top of the desk.

The judge walked over.

Confused, astonished, but silent.

Then Rikki entered the room, just as confused and astonished as her father.

"What's that?"

"It might be the gun that killed Edward Colt," I explained.

"I thought Eric killed Edward," she said.

"I never believed that."

"How did it get there?" she wondered.

I ignored her.

"Did you ever see it before?"

"No, of course not."

Her father, nodding his agreement, stated the obvious.

"Someone's been in the house."

"When?" Rikki wondered.

"Maybe when you were both at the wake," I said. "Maybe earlier."

"What does it mean?" her father asked.

"It means that someone is trying to implicate Rikki."

"Which means she's still in danger," her father said. "Correct?"

"Correct."

He thought it over quickly.

"I want you to take her with you."

"I was planning on it. I'll be back tomorrow around noon."

I pulled my cell, took pictures of the Beretta, and texted the picture and the serial number to Nonna. Then I dialed for Dawson.

As I waited for Dawson to pick up, I looked at the worried father who put his arm around his daughter's shoulders. Protectively.

He had one daughter left, and he wasn't asking much of me: just solve two murders (one ten years cold) and protect his only remaining child.

23

The Barrens

Saturday, March 28th
40°

I WAS CRUISING THROUGH Kallikak country.

Quite possibly the weirdest part of the weirdest state.

Although some would argue with that.

The Pine Barrens are a National Reserve (being the first one in the nation, I might add), covering over a million acres of rural, backwoods, mostly unpopulated pine (and cedar, laurel, dogwood, and oak) forests, occupying over twenty percent of the most densely populated state in the union. Larger than Yosemite. Larger than Grand Canyon National Park.

It's an ecological oddity, covering huge chunks of seven South Jersey counties, providing much of the water for the Cohansey-Kirkwood Aquifer, a fantastic underground reservoir of seventeen trillion gallons of the purest cleanest water in America.

The Barrens are chock full of swamps, carnivorous plants, and Kallikaks.

Not to mention the Jersey Devil.

In 1920, the distinguished psychologist Henry H. Goddard published his famous study, *The Kallikak Family*, about a huge extended Piney family consisting of inbreds, bastards, imbeciles, prostitutes, illiterates, drunks, syphilitics, arsonists, paupers, and thieves. The book was universally praised in all the most important elite and academic circles, and it suggested that the Kallikaks, and everyone like them, should be immediately sterilized and institutionalized.

But there were a few problems.

Not the least of which was that H. H. Goddard was a quack. He was one of those self-important, racist, pseudo-science eugenicists, whom the Nazis would later come to admire so much. He not only cheated his "evidence," but he even doctored his photographs. As for the so-called Kallikak family, that wasn't even their real name, and they were apparently from distant Hunterdon County, not the Pine Barrens.

But stuff like that feeds on itself.

The following year, another influential "researcher," Elizabeth Kite, published a report called "The Pineys," castigating everybody in the Barrens as inbred, incestuous drunks. The governor got so spooked about the "race of imbeciles, criminals, and defectives" living within his garden state that he wanted the legislature to "isolate" the "menace," although I'm not exactly sure how he intended to quarantine twenty-two percent of the state, thus creating a state-within-a-state for wild incestuous imbeciles.

The truth is, most of the Pineys I've met are just like the rest of us Jerseyites, just much more rural, much more country.

At the moment, my Caddie XTS was cruising through the deserted backwoods of Mullica Township within the heart of the Pines. I was searching for a street called Pine Ridge Lane. Street number unknown. Eventually, my GPS lady stopped talking, as if suddenly swallowed up by a clan of Kallikaks, so I reverted to my Rand McNally.

I prefer maps anyway.

After my fourth left turn on the fourth houseless and homeless dirt road, I noticed an old wooden sign that had "Piney Ridge Boulevard" scrawled across it.

I guess everybody in New Jersey has to be a wiseass, even the inbreds.

I drove up a winding dirt road, surrounded by pines and cedars, the only things hardy enough to grow in the acidic "sugar sand" of the Barrens. Around a narrow bend, I came upon a little shack, which might or might not have been somebody's home, with a little log cabin further up the ridge. As I approached the cabin, a big ole boy came out of the shack and stepped in the middle of the dirt road, as if he'd been waiting to intercept me all day long. He had a Browning A-Bolt shotgun, which he was holding by the barrel, with the butt down in the dust, and an ugly four-legged creature that looked like a cross between a hound and a pit.

I wondered if I'd have to kill the thing.

I got out of my car, trying to ignore the dust at my feet.

I tried to be civil.

Why not?

"I'm looking for Kitty Walsh," I said, assuming she was in the log cabin on the ridge.

"You need to go back where you came from."

He was firm, but oddly polite.

When I walked up to him, his dog growled.

I don't own a dog, but I don't actively dislike them. I realize that, for some people, they're the only friends and companions they'll ever have. But nasty growling dogs are a menace, and I have no problem with—what's the euphemism?—"putting them down."

"Am I going to have to kill that thing?"

The big boy understood.

He tapped his best pal on the top of its head, and the growling stopped immediately. When the thing looked up at its lord and master, the big boy nodded towards home sweet home, and the thing, very reluctantly, strolled over to the shack, went inside, then turned around to look back at his boss.

The big boy nodded his head, and the beast, using its ugly head, shut the front door. I was very impressed, but I didn't drive out here in the middle of nowhere for a circus act.

"Thanks," I said, fully aware that we were both fully aware that I was being a hundred percent sarcastic.

The big boy had definitely noticed the bulge under my Armani, and he seemed willing to be reasonable.

I identified myself and my mission.

"I'm a private detective, and I need to talk to Kitty Walsh about the death of her daughter."

"She's already talked about it with that other cop."

Meaning Edward Colt.

Which I already knew.

It was why Edward had added Kitty's name to Pavese's suspect list.

"I just need a few minutes," I tried, trying not to lose my patience.

"You know," he said, almost philosophically, "I'm fully aware that to a slick-looking guido like yourself, I look very much like the Piney stereotype, but I'm a very reasonable man."

I was always grateful when I was misidentified as a paisan.

It made my day.

Now why in the world would I ever think this guy might fit some kind of stereotype? (Even though he'd just stereotyped me.) After all, he was almost six foot five, with worn flannels, worn dungarees, worn work boots, an ugly beard, a stupid tattoo, and a man-eating hound of the Baskervilles.

He continued his moving soliloquy.

"My sister's put the past behind her, and she won't want to talk to you or anyone else."

I guess he was *really* trying to be reasonable.

Just with the wrong guy.

"Why don't you go back inside your Unabomber shack."

I couldn't help adding:

"Pardon the stereotype."

He'd had enough.

He knew I was carrying a handgun, but he also figured that he could put an end to things pretty quickly. He dropped the barrel of his shotgun and grabbed for me with his right hand. Much quicker than I would have expected.

To be honest about it, I would have preferred to tase the guy and watch him jerk around in the sugar sand. After all, the big ones are always the most fun, but there simply wasn't enough time.

There's a myriad of methodologies to put an end to these kinds of confrontations, since there are so many, shall we say, human vulnerabilities. As for me, I've used them all, except for the "man area."

No thanks.

I stepped to my right and struck him in the throat and crushed his windpipe. I used a more moderate "hand blow" rather than a "knuckle blow" because I didn't want to kill the guy. Trachea strikes are extremely effective. The throat is pretty much all cartilage, and getting your Adam's apple crushed back into your esophagus hurts like hell.

From what I understand, it's a rather exquisite pain.

The big boy gagged, rather disgustingly, then slumped forward, falling to his knees, clutching his throat. He made a futile effort to scream, but nothing much came out. It was like looking at Munch's "Scream" in a silent Oslo Art Gallery.

A few minutes later, I knocked on Kitty's door. The little cabin was very neat, well kept, even "cute," with bright colorful flowers in all the flower boxes.

"Go away."

It came through the door.

There was no chance of that.

"Would you like your brother back?"

The door opened a crack.

"What does that mean?"

She wasn't happy about it.

"Let me come inside."

She thought it over. Then she decided I was a serious man.

Wisely.

She opened the door. She was wearing a pretty green sundress, and she was obviously weaponless, although there was a fully loaded gun rack on the far wall. O'Brien might have burned all her pictures twenty-seven years ago, but Nonna had found one from about ten years back, when she looked a lot like the young Sissy Spacek, with light brown hair, freckled fair skin, with something both "little girlish" and, contradictorily, "sultryish" about her. These days, she looked a bit used and worn out, like heavy-duty smokers usually do, even though she was only thirty-four.

"Where's my brother?"

"He's in the trunk of my car."

She looked at me closely, wondering if I might be capable of such of thing. Not whether I might be capable of locking someone inside my trunk, but whether I might be capable of subduing her gargantuan brother one-on-one.

I guess she decided I was.

"Did you hurt him?"

"No."

Which wasn't *exactly* the truth since he'll be sipping soup for the next month and a half.

She seemed to read my mind, so I beat her to the punch.

"Call him."

"I should call the police."

I wasn't worried.

She walked over to her sitting chair, picked up her cell, and called her brother.

Which gave me a little time to look around.

She kept the place neat. Very lovely.

I like neatness.

I'm not a compulsive, but I'm *very* neat. "Neat" in the *full* sense of the word. Not just wearing neat, carefully ironed, lint-free suits and having a McDonald's wrapper-free car. The *truly* neat person understands that it's a three-part affair: the physical world around us, the body we boss around, and the command center itself—the mush within our skulls we call our brains.

Our minds.

Which, of course, is the hardest part to keep in order.

I walked over and sat down on Kitty's couch. She was also sitting, talking to her brother, who was a bit "tied up" at the moment.

"Where *are* you?"

I heard him eke out the word "trunk," confirming my allegations.

She hung up the phone, glaring across her red Persian rug. I was glad that her rifles were safely on the wall behind me.

Before she could say something unpleasant, I spoke first.

"Just answer a few questions, and I'll be gone."

Like her brother, she could be "reasonable," and that seemed to be the best course of action at the moment.

"I've already answered all the questions. Ten years ago, and last week with some nice cop."

"He's dead."

If she was surprised, she didn't show it. Kitty wasn't about to reveal anything she didn't have to.

"He was much nicer than you," she insisted.

"Most people are."

Actually, I think I'm a very nice person, but two people were dead, and one was her daughter, and I refused to quibble about it.

"What do you want to know?"

She wanted her big brother out of my trunk, but I acted as if I had nothing but time.

I looked around the room, carefully, then I asked her a question I knew the answer to.

"How much does O'Brien give you?"

"That's none of your business."

Then she thought about her brother's claustrophobic predicament, and she made an effort to cooperate.

"Enough," she assured me.

"He keeps you comfortable."

"He keeps *all* of his women comfortable."

Which got me interested.

"Like whom?"

"Like, screw you!"

I guess it was time to get to the heart of the matter.

"I know you were at the bowling alley that night."

She was surprised, even impressed, and she didn't attempt to deny it.

"I'd tried to see the twins a number of times before that night," she shrugged, "but they never responded. So I followed Nikki and her friends from the promenade."

"Why?"

She shrugged again, as if she couldn't really comprehend her own maternal urges.

"I wanted to help. Somehow. In some way. And I did."

She seemed proud of herself.

"How?"

"By telling her that I wanted to help her."

She was attempting, not very cleverly, to be evasive.

"By giving her permission," I said.

She was shocked and angry.

"You can leave now, mister" she said.

Which I took to be a "yes."

I stood up, walked to the door, and turned for one more question.

"Why Nikki and not Rikki?"

She shrugged, as if her two offspring were essentially interchangeable, and I believed her shrug.

Outside, I immediately texted Xander, my computer kid, and left him a message. Since I already had my phone out, I checked to see if Roxs had sent her daily message. Not yet. So I checked her text from a month ago.

Heading to Monument Valley. Looking for the Ringo Kid.

We'd watched *Stagecoach* together with my uncle. That was about two months ago, which now seemed like a million years ago.

A world ago.

She smiled and said:

"Wow, John Wayne was *really* handsome!"

Of course, he was.

I walked to my car, ignoring the four-legged creature howling inside the wooden shack, and opened the trunk.

24

Cheesequake

Saturday, March 28th
42°

S INATRA AGAIN:

> *You go to my head. . . .*

Well, maybe she was.

> *You linger like a haunting refrain. . . .*

She was lingering beside me, wearing a preppy red Rutgers polo, tight new jeans, and cute leather moccasins. Looking hyper-nerdy, collegiate, perfect, beautiful beyond comprehensibility, and delicious (am I allowed to say that?).

We were sitting in the front of a rented black SUV, cruising up the Garden State Parkway, the central nervous system of the greatest state in the union.

Who doesn't want to live in New Jersey?

The highest cost of living.

The highest property taxes.

The most traffic congestion.

The most racehorses (sorry Kentucky).

The most diners.

The first brewery.

The first submarine (Paterson, NJ)

The first baseball game.

The first seaplane.

The first light bulb.

The first record player.

The first electric guitar.

The first medical center.

The first drive-in.

The first radio station (Paterson, NJ).

The first boardwalk.

The first college football game.

The longest boardwalk.

The largest seaport in America.

Etc., etc.

She shut off the Chairman of the Board.
I tried not to let it ruin my perfect day.
"Tell me about Jack Colt," she said.

I glanced over at She-Who-Must-Be-Obeyed.

"What you see is what you get."

She seemed dissatisfied, so I tried another tack.

"*You* tell me."

She did, gladly, telling me about myself.

Happily.

"You're eerily famous, you're a reputed tough guy, and you're absolutely full of yourself."

I considered interrupting so I could refute the third and harshest of her characterizations, but I decided to let it go.

"You bailed on football at Rutgers U, for some unknown reason, where you majored in two 'first-rate' career choices: philosophy and film."

"Cinema," I corrected.

She ignored me.

"Somehow you survived Seton Hall Law, did some prosecuting in Paterson, then joined your uncle's PI firm in downtown Paterson. You live on a big hill called Garrett Mountain with all your friends. Meaning you live alone. You've messed up all your relationships with the superior sex, which is why, incidentally, I'll never bother to get involved, and you're also a health nut, somehow subsisting on pizza, White Castle, fajitas, baked ziti, and diner omelettes. To compensate, you do sprints and beat a heavy bag."

"Somebody's been talking to Nonna."

"I guess somebody's a detective."

Is it possible to resist a wiseass Jersey girl?

"Anything else?"

"Yeah, she assured me that although you *always* wear the same exact clothes, it's a new set every day, since you've got over twenty duplicates of the same Armani suit, the same Brooks Brothers shirt, and the same Florsheims. So despite the 'beautiful mind' weirdness of it all, it's quite a relief to know that you actually change your clothes."

"Your 'relief' has always been my prime directive."

"She also says that you're thirty-two, nocturnal, and that nobody knows what color your eyes are since you've been wearing those stupid shades since you were a toddler."

"That's a gross exaggeration."

"What color are they?"

"Brown."

She seemed pleased with herself.

"I didn't know beach girls were such wiseasses."

"There's a lot you don't know, Jack Colt."

I didn't argue with her. Besides, it was time for one of her non sequiturs.

"I'm hungry."

She said it like a child, as if she hadn't eaten in three days.

"Have some fudge."

She found the box on the back seat, and she took a piece.

"Where are we going?"

"Somerville."

"Why?"

"So I can get out of this car and talk to someone else."

The real reason was that Nonna had tracked down the serial number to a gun stolen in Somerville.

"Mrs. Salerno also told me that you lost your parents when you were a kid and that you never talk about it."

She was serious.

"I was ten months old."

"Tell me about it."

Why do I always do what pretty girls want?

I told her.

"They were killed in a car crash. North of here on the Parkway, near exit 157."

"I'm sorry."

"When the paramedics got there, Sinatra was still singing."

She seemed confused for a moment, then less so.

She pointed at the console.

"The same CD?"

"Yeah. My uncle gave it to me when I was thirteen. He thought I could handle it."

"Was he right?"

"Yes."

By now, I'd pulled into the Cheesequake Service Area at Mile 123, parking in an isolated part of the parking lot, not far from the multifarious culinary palaces: Burger King, Sbarro's, Nathan's, etc. Even a Starbucks for the liquid-challenged.

I looked over at the pretty girl sitting beside me.

"I've never told anyone that before."

"The Sinatra CD?"

"Yeah, the Sinatra CD."

"Thank you, Jack."

She meant it.

"Now I need to tell you some things about ten years ago."

"All right."

She seemed ready, and there was no reason to beat around the bush.

"Two days after Nikki and Billy met on the promenade, they were married in Delaware."

I let it sink in for a moment.

Then I explained what happened. How two silly young kids had met on the promenade, how they'd fallen in love, how they met up later that night, deciding, inexplicably, to get married as soon as possible. But there was a problem, Nikki was only seventeen. She needed parental permission.

Besides there was a twenty-four hour waiting period.

After staying up all night, they drove to the Pines early the next morning and convinced Kitty Walsh, the mother, who was glad to help, to sign the permission form. The next day, they took the ferry to Lewes, took a cab to the office of the County Clerk of Peace in Georgetown, and got themselves married.

Later that night, they took the ferry back to Cape May, tried to get Billy a room at the Gingerbread, which was already full, so they went over to the Queen Victoria. They were probably planning to tell Rikki and her father the next day, but, of course, Nikki ended up dead later that night.

Rikki sat there, staring at the console.

"Are you sure about this, Jack?"

"Yes."

I tried to be delicate.

"Was Nikki the impulsive type?"

"No, not at all, Jack. I'm shocked."

"Are you shocked that she didn't tell you first?"

"Yes."

"Would you have done such a thing yourself?"

"I can't imagine it, but, of course, I really can't know. Right?"

She looked at me, then asked another question.

"Is 'love at first sight' really real?"

"Yes."

She shrugged.

"What happened to Billy?"

"I don't know. I'm guessing that he woke up the next morning, and everyone was talking about the Cove Beach murder. I'm guessing that he realized that he'd be the main suspect, so he took off. Leaving town. I have no idea where he went, but he never showed up again in North Jersey."

"He's my brother-in-law."

She seemed amazed by the idea.

"Yes."

"Did he kill my sister?"

"I don't know."

25

Somerville

Saturday, March 28th
45°

THE OLD LADY INSISTED on "tea and shortbread cookies," and I didn't have the heart to tell her how ridiculous it sounded.

Three years ago, when her husband, Bruno Vitelli, a retired Somerville cop, died of heart failure, someone came to the post-burial reception at their home and stole his service revolver from a drawer upstairs in the master bedroom. It was the same Beretta 92 that had killed Edward Colt and ended up in Nikki's desk drawer.

I thought I should be polite.

"I'm a huge Van Cleef fan."

The widow, Mrs. Wendy Vitelli, was perfectly delighted, as she held out the cookie tray.

Being a gentleman, I took one.

She was sixty or so, plumpish, terminally friendly, and she kept a cozy comfortable house.

"We're very proud of him," she said, "and his memory."

"Did you ever meet him?"

Since I knew I'd never get out of the house without trying one of her homemades, I took a small bite of the bland-looking shortbread, and I was astonished how good it tasted. I looked down at the tray, now on the coffee table, and I counted the cookies. There were three of us in the room—me, Mrs. Vitelli, and Rikki—and five remaining cookies, which meant that, given Rikki's weight and exacting trimness, I could probably end up with three, if not four.

"I knew his cousins, but I only saw him once when he came back to town one time. I was a young girl back then, and he was as nice as a man could be nice, but he still scared me to death!"

Since I was being so polite, I looked over at Rikki and tried to explain what we were talking about.

"Lee Van Cleef was the greatest badass in film history, and he grew up here in Somerville."

Rikki was interested, but she needed some help, and Mrs. Vitelli tried to prompt her.

"Have you ever seen any of those spaghetti westerns, my dear?"

Rikki didn't have a clue.

"*The Good, the Bad, and the Ugly*," I tried.

Rikki shook her head in the negative, as I'd fully anticipated.

"How about *High Noon*?" I tried, thinking it might have a chance.

"With Gary Cooper?"

"Yes, dearie. Lee was one of the outlaws. He had a lovely heart in real life, but the dear Lord gave him sinister looks."

I tried to conjure a visual.

"He had cold piercing eyes, super-high cheekbones, and a hawklike nose. He was also lean and mean. I loved the guy."

"I thought you hated bad guys?" Rikki kidded.

"Only in real life."

As casually as possible, I took another cookie, and no one seemed to notice.

It was time to get to the gun.

"How many people came after the burial?"

"The place was packed. I was naturally distraught and teary, but I did my best to be welcoming, and I appreciated all the nice tributes to Bruno. We were very close. Married for thirty-four happy years."

I felt sorry for the old woman, and Rikki, sitting next to her on the living room couch, placed a comforting hand over the widow's hand.

"Were there people there you didn't know?"

"Yes. Bruno knew everyone in town, and we both have lots of relatives."

I took out the pictures and handed them to the widow.

"I know it was three years ago, but I'd appreciate it if you could take a look."

She did.

Carefully.

They were my "suspect photos," most of which were pictures of the girls and Tommy, etc., way back at the time of the murder.

She took her time.

Then she stopped at one, looking at me across the tantalizing tray of shortbreads.

Amazed.

"Is that Veronica Miller?"

"Yes."

I was equally amazed.

"How do you know her?"

"She's a cousin of mine. Once removed. On the Scottish side."

Thus the shortbread.

"Was she there that day?"

"I can't remember. I don't think so."

I tried to prompt her.

"No redheads?"

I knew it was a lot to ask a grieving widow to remember something like that from three years ago.

"There *was* a redhead," she remembered, "but I only saw her from a distance. Maybe it was Ronnie."

Rikki, Ronnie's best friend, was stunned and silent.

I have to admit, I was also taken back a bit.

26

Fairmount

R IKKI STOOD in the cemetery and cried.

Maybe it wasn't such a good idea.

Two nights ago on the beach, I'd asked her about lots of stuff, including her job. I wondered why a registered nurse would prefer to work as an EMT. There's a definite hierarchy in the nursing world, just like everywhere else in the world, with nurses at the top, paramedics in the middle, and EMT's at the lower end.

"I like the action," she said, simply. "Something you'd probably understand."

I did, but she elaborated anyway.

"There's plenty of desperation in the hospitals, and I enjoyed all my rotations at Cape Regional—surgery, pediatrics, psychiatrics, ER, maternity—but I always wanted to 'save' people, not just 'help' them, and when you're out on the road, it's very often life-and-deathish. A matter of minutes."

I understood.

"So I gave up my hospital position and went back on the street. Nurses are licensed, and paramedics are certified, but I was both.

Most people don't realize that nurses aren't allowed to intubate, do trachs, or do pericardial taps. But since I was also a para, I could do it all, and it's come in handy. Very handy."

Sometimes, in my own sketchy life, I like to justify everything I do as essentially "good," given my overall intentions. Justice. Protection. Stuff like that. But this young woman had been saving lives ever since she was a teenager.

"It's what we always wanted to do."

The two of them.

The Bobbseys.

"I saw the picture of Clara on your wall."

She was impressed.

"You know the story?"

"I've been to her grave."

"Wow, I've always wanted to go there."

I liked the sincerity of her "wow."

She looked at me with a look that I would have to define as innocently seductive.

"Maybe you could take me sometime."

"Are you flirting with your father's hired hand?"

She smiled.

"Maybe I am."

After tea time with Wendy was a wrap, I hit 287, then took 78 east into Newark. I know every single inch of Paterson, but I also know Newark very well. After all, I went to law school in Newark, and I knew that we could make a quick stop at the cemetery before we drove north to Newton.

Uncertain what to do, I stepped over next to her and put my arm gently around her shoulders. Maybe it was a mistake, but my life is littered with mistakes.

"She was our hero when we were little girls," she said. "She was everything we wanted to be."

Excepting Clara Barton, Clara Maass was the most famous nurse in American history, and, of course, a Jersey girl from Newark. Back in 1898, when the Spanish-American War broke out, she left her hospital position in Newark and volunteered to serve, ending up in both the Philippines and Cuba, taking on all the big-boy killers: typhoid, malaria, dengue, and the killer of all killers, yellow fever.

Known as "yellow jack."

In 1901, she was down in Cuba with Walter Reed trying to figure out how the "jack" was being transmitted. The suspicion that it might be mosquito borne was proving impossible to verify, so Clara and several others volunteered to infect themselves.

She survived the first time, but not the second.

It put an end to all "human" medical experiments in the US, but it *did* prove the mosquito theory, and it led to the near eradication of the yellow jack in Cuba and, subsequently, in all the Americas, saving millions of lives.

She'd sacrificed her own life for others.

Eventually, they brought her back home to Newark and lay her in the grave beneath us. They also renamed the Newark German Hospital the Clara Maass Medical Center, now located in Belleville, where my uncle was once treated for a gunshot wound.

"What's with the crybaby stuff?" I kidded, gently. "I thought it's what you wanted."

She turned and looked at me, right through my shades, right into my eyes.

"You're too stupid to understand."

Maybe I was.

I like to believe that I "understand" females more than most other guys, but the truth is, I don't have a clue.

She smiled.

It was a smile that I'd like to see a lot more of.

27

Sussex County Courthouse

Saturday, March 28th
45°

S HE WAS LOOKING pretty good.

Better than I remembered.

Rita Sehorn was a young prosecutor at the Newton Courthouse, in the north country. The last and only time I'd seen her was at some stupid lawyers reception at the Brownstone in Paterson. We talked a bit, but when she got a bit loopy on the Chardonnay, she looked at me with a pair of mushy "want to" eyes, and I got the hell out of there.

At the moment, she was sitting on the front steps of the old courthouse at High and Spring Streets, seemingly perfectly content, with a little notebook on her lap, and a pen in her hand. She was wearing a lovely green blouse, with a white knit sweater, and a pair of deadly black spikes. She was dirty blonde, neat, attractive, smart, and looking a bit like Helen Hunt.

When she looked up, she saw the last person on earth she expected to see. Me.

"Jack?"

She placed her notebook on the step beside her and stood up. It was definitely awkward time. Do we shake hands, or hug (I'm not much for that), or just stand there awkward as hell? I preempted the problem by putting out my hand. She shook it like a dear old friend.

"What's the city boy doing up here in the country?"

I didn't think it was fair to beat around the bush.

"I've been hired by Richard O'Brien to give the Nikki O'Brien murder another look."

She was surprised.

"Why you, Jack?"

"He thinks I'm good."

"Well, you are, Jack, but that's a long time ago."

"Yeah, ten years ago."

"Can we sit? I'm on break from some stupid, ball-buster case, and I always come out here to wash away my mind."

We sat down on the steps, beneath the six huge columns of the old historic courthouse.

"You were pals with Nikki and Rikki," I started.

"I was. *Close* pals. Everybody loved them back then."

"Did your mom?"

She was surprised, and she smiled.

"You *are* good, Jack."

Then she answered my question.

"For some reason, my mom was always foolishly competitive. I was her only kid, and she wanted me to be first at everything, not second, certainly not third, but I didn't mind. What's so bad about being third?"

When I didn't respond, she remembered.

"Besides, my mom always found them a little 'too good to

be true.' But she didn't know the twins like I did. Yeah, they were goody-goody and goofy, but no one cared, because they were such a lot of fun and such good friends. True friends. Loyal friends."

"Where's your mom these days?"

Rita knew when "the likes of me" was asking about a suspect, but she didn't seem to mind.

"She died five years ago. She was visiting relatives in Tacoma, Washington, and she had a heart attack."

"Were you close?"

"Yes, my father died when I was five. All we had was each other."

She smiled again, but it wasn't a "come on," and I was relieved.

"You got any more rude, much-too-personal questions, Jack?"

"Yeah, tell me about your husband."

"We're separated."

The sadness was real.

Intense.

"You're still wearing your ring."

She looked down at her wedding band.

"Yeah, it's hard to give things up sometimes."

I understood.

I also noticed the pen she was holding. It had a little red martlet on it.

She changed the subject.

"I think I owe you an apology, Jack."

"I doubt that."

"I think I got a little drunk at the Brownstone that night. Casey had left me, and I guess I was lonely."

I assumed that Casey was her husband.

"We're all lonely, Rita."

She nodded, then she left her apology right where it was.

Rikki walked up.

I'd told her to give me ten minutes alone with Rita because I didn't want their mutual past getting in the way of my questions.

Rita looked up.

She was stunned.

Happily stunned.

She stood right up, and the two young women hugged in a way that only women who are very close friends can embrace each other.

My cell vibrated, so I walked down the street towards the new courthouse and left the two of them alone. They were jabbering away, like the best of friends, like teenagers.

I check Nonna's text. There was no message, just the DMV photo of William Kelly from over ten years ago.

Maybe I should have been surprised.

But I wasn't.

28

18 Marshall Street

Saturday, March 28th
43°

A s REQUESTED, Mrs. Doris Salerno, aka Nonna, had all the obituaries laid out neatly on my office desk, and the three of us looked them over: me, Nonna, and her new best friend Rikki.

The obits were for all the funeral parlor viewings in the North Jersey/Kinnelon area that took place during the three days that Edward Colt claimed that he was going to Harrisburg, Pennsylvania, when his phone was actually pinging in North Jersey.

As expected, there were no "Colts" on the table, but I did come across a "Mary Montgomery," who'd been the "loving mother of Sean 'Sonny' (deceased) and Jennie Montgomery Asher of Morristown, New Jersey"

My two co-detectives read the obit over my shoulder.

"I wonder, sweetheart," Nonna said to Rikki, "if Sonny boy was jealous of Billy."

I could see that this was her new method of busting my balls: talking to Rikki and pretending that I was too dumb to understand. Or that I wasn't in the room. Or that I didn't exist at all.

I decided to play along.

Addressing Rikki:

"Yes, sweetheart, I believe that we considered that hyper-obvious possibility several days ago."

"That's odd," Rikki said, as if ignoring the both of us. "The same night that Nikki and the kids were together at the lighthouse, I was at home reading a novel about jealousy. About a particularly obsessive kind of jealously."

"What was it?" I asked.

"*The End of the Affair.*"

I wanted to say "great book"—actually, one of the best of the last century—but I stayed on course.

"I thought you were reading *Persuasion?*"

She looked at me with mock-frustration. Like I was a moron. So did Nonna, who *always* looked at me like I was a moron.

"After I finished reading *Persuasion* that night, I started on Graham Greene."

She turned to Nonna.

"How could anyone love such a silly and suspicious man?"

Which gave Nonna the perfect opening.

"None ever have, and none ever will. Both he and his Lenny-like best friend, who claims to be my grandson, have a long history of relationship disasters. I honestly have no idea how Luca finally found the woman he did. She's oddly lovely, but I think she might also be retarded."

Although appreciating the allusion to *Of Mice and Men*, I felt obligated to defend Luca's marvelous wife.

"I hope Gina never hears you say that."

"I've already told her."

I gave up.

I had a murder to solve.

Two of them.

"If I had a competent assistant," I said to Rikki, "I'd ask her to get me the contact info on Jennie Asher."

The old goat looked at Rikki.

"You know, honey, I get combat pay for working here. Three times what I'm worth. The truth is, he's as inept with money as he is with women."

Rikki laughed.

So did I.

Nonna looked suspiciously at Rikki.

"You're not falling for him, are you?"

Rikki took her rudeness right in stride.

"I'm trying not to."

"Try harder."

Then Nonna went into her reception room, sat down at her desk, and started clicking away at her computer.

"She's a piece of work," I whispered to Rikki.

"I heard that!" the Insult-Grandma called out from the next room.

Rikki laughed again, sitting down in my "client" chair and looking at all the autographed photos framed on the wall: the Jersey singers, the NFL linebackers.

From Frank Sinatra to Ray Nitschke.

"It's like sitting in a little boy's bedroom," she kidded.

"Got that right!" Nonna called out.

No man can *ever* get the upper hand with a wisenheimer woman, let alone two of them, so I muted myself.

Nonna was back.

"She runs a florist shop in Bloomfield. Here's her number."

"Good job. Your bonus is in the mail."

Immediately, before she had a chance to respond, I stepped into my uncle's office. When I shut the door behind me, I could hear them whispering like Roman conspirators, but I didn't pay any attention.

Before I dialed the number, Dawson texted:

No prints on the Beretta.

I wasn't surprised, and I'm sure Dawson wasn't either.

I dialed Sonny's sister.

"Asher's Flowers. How can I help?"

"Is this Jennie Asher?"

"Yes, it is."

She seemed pleasant.

"I'm Jack Colt. I'm a private investigator looking for Billy Kelly, and I'm hoping you can help me."

I was on my best behavior. I really didn't want to drive to Morristown tonight unless it was absolutely necessary.

"I doubt I'll be able to help. I haven't seen Billy in ten years."

"Didn't he show up at your mother's wake?"

"No."

I was surprised.

"Are you sure?"

"Yes."

Maybe he didn't want to be seen.

Maybe he went to the funeral and sat in the back.

Maybe he went to the cemetery.

"Jennie, I'm sending you a photo of Billy. Can you can confirm that it's him?"

It was Billy's motor vehicles photo.

I waited.

"That's him. I'm sure of it. He and my older brother were best friends."

"What happened?"

"I don't know. I heard that Billy dropped out of college and hit the road."

"Where?"

"Sonny once said that he was probably in Europe."

"Why?"

"'Cause he talked about it a lot when they were kids."

I tried to be tactful.

"I understand that Sonny died five years ago."

"That's correct."

"How did he die?"

"It was an industrial accident. He was working in a cable factory."

"Which one?"

"I don't know. In Paterson somewhere. I'm sorry, but I need to get back to work. We're overloaded with orders to fill."

"Just one more question. Did you ever hear of Edward Colt?"

She seemed confused.

"I thought that was *you*."

"I'm Jack Colt. Thanks for your time."

I went back into my office and looked at Nonna. The kidding was over, and she knew it.

"I want you to check out Rita's marriage to Casey Sehorn. Both here and in Canada."

"Canada?" she asked, not expecting an answer.

"Yeah, she was using a pen today with a little red martlet on it."

"What's that?" Rikki wondered.

"The mascot at McGill University."

Nonna nodded.

She liked to complain a lot, but she also enjoyed all the difficult searches. The challenges.

"What about Izzy? Did you find her yet?"

"Not yet, but I'm getting closer."

"I need to talk to her tonight. We'll go over to Stone House and wait."

She was fine with that.

As for Rikki, she was enjoying herself.

"I like being a detective."

29

Stone House

WHEN SHE CAME BACK into the room, I put the book on the table. When people think about Shakespeare and jealousy, they naturally think about *Othello*, but there's also *Cymbeline* and *The Winter's Tale*.

I was rereading the latter.

It's about some pea-brain king named Leontes, who decides that his best friend is having an affair with his wife, so he puts out a "hit" on his best friend and throws his virtuous wife in prison, where she dies. But hell, it's not really a "tragedy," because, after five acts, it all ends perfectly happily with a back-from-the-dead miracle and a party-down. It's certainly not one of his best, but he doesn't hesitate to characterize the absolute insanity of what the shrinks call "delusional jealousy," what other people call "Othello Syndrome," even though I'm not buying that General O actually had the O Syndrome. He got conned into thinking Desdemona was unfaithful. He didn't just conjure it out of thin air like an idiot, like Leontes; he was a gullible moron who got cleverly duped by Iago.

I looked at my house guest and thought how easily a man could get deluded about her.

Or, I suppose, her dead sister.

While we were waiting for Nonna's text, Rikki was enjoying herself, checking the place out. Stone House, made of stone, sat at the top of Garrett Mountain, overlooking the night-lights of Paterson. It was small, neat, comfortable, and clean, with lots of wood and even more stone.

"I like it," she decided, "despite the hypermasculinity."

"It was built back when Lambert built his castle, in 1892, and no woman has ever lived here. Never."

It was a sad fact, but it was still a fact.

The place had been inhabited by a long line of womanless, wifeless Colts, passing down, eventually, to my uncle.

Now to me.

Rikki understood.

She glanced down at *The Winter's Tale* but didn't comment.

"Show me your Paterson," she said.

Her wish was my command.

We walked through the back of the house to the outside porch, five hundred feet over the base of the mountain. Below us, the lights of the city were beautiful.

As always.

As were the distant lights of the New York City skyline.

"Where are the falls?"

I pointed down below, off to the right, at the Paterson Falls.

She said nothing, fully aware that my uncle had been assassinated there last month. Forty-three days ago.

"Why not tell me a Colt story?"

Why not?

So I told her how Hamilton's vision of a great industrial city, powered by the waterfall, had come to fruition, with its numerous mills and numerous factories. Then Sam Colt came down from Connecticut, set up his arms factory, and developed a prototype called "The Paterson," a single-action revolver, that later morphed into the Colt Walker, then the even more famous Colt 45, "the gun that tamed the West."

"The Walker?"

"Yeah, Sam Walker was a captain in the Texas Rangers, and he got together with Sam Colt, and they took the Paterson and they turned it into the largest, most powerful handgun in the world. Walker wanted lots of 'firepower,' and he got it. The gun was used by the Rangers and by the military in the Mexican War. It remained the most powerful handgun in the world until 1935, when the .357 Magnum came on the market."

She looked down at my city.

I had no idea what she was thinking about.

After all, does a man ever *really* know what a woman is thinking about?

She turned and looked at me directly.

"You're a very strange person, Jack Colt."

I think it was supposed to be a compliment of some kind, but I wasn't sure. To be honest, I never thought I was "strange" at all.

But maybe I was.

She kissed me on the mouth.

Like cotton candy at the Jersey Shore.

Like heaven.

When it was over, she smiled mischievously.

"I shouldn't have done that. Forget about it."

"Not very likely."

"I'm very vulnerable right now."

I didn't know what to say.

"Besides, Nikki made me do it."

Now, I *really* didn't know what to say.

She stepped over to the porch bench and sat down in the moonlight. Looking lovely. Looking (oh, the hell with it, why not use the b-word?) beautiful.

She attempted to explain herself.

"She's with me all the time, Jack. Every minute of every day. Can you understand that?"

"Not really. Maybe in theory."

"Do you ever talk to yourself?"

"Sometimes. Not much."

"Well, I talk to Nikki all the time, and she talks right back, and she always encourages me, and she said, 'Kiss the big boy,' so I did."

"It sounds to me like you're denying culpability."

She laughed.

"Of course, I am."

Of course, I was even more confused than before. Even more attracted.

"Will she be prompting you again in the near future?"

"I think she thinks we both need a temporary moratorium."

I liked the redundant word "temporary." Then I changed the subject.

"Can you handle some more cold case stuff?"

"Yes."

I sat down beside her.

I wanted to hold her hand, but I didn't.

"It's a little weird, Rikki."

"Tell me."

"Edward Colt *was* Billy Kelly."

She was amazed. Stunned, but not upset.

"Are you sure?"

"Yes."

"I thought he was nearly forty?"

"He lied about his age when he created his new identity."

She thought about it for a moment.

"Which means he was my brother-in-law."

"Yes."

"Which means I dated my own brother-in-law!"

"Yes."

"Which he knew."

"Yes."

"You're right, Jack, it *is* creepy. *Very* creepy."

I made an effort to de-creepy it.

"I'm sure he found you irresistible."

"Just like my sister?"

"Yes."

She thought it over, so I kept moving things along.

"It's probably why he hadn't interviewed Ronnie yet. Or Rita. Or Izzy. He knew that they'd recognize him."

"Then the cat would be out of the bag."

"Yes."

Then she asked me the same question that she'd asked me this morning in the Cheesequake service area.

"Did he kill my sister?"

"I don't know, Rikki. But I don't think so. I have the feeling that he came back to Cape May to try and solve the murder and clear his name."

My cell vibrated.
Finally.
"Go ahead," she said.
I read Nonna's text.
"Can you tell me?"
"Sure."
I read her the text:

Izzy's a dealer at the Borgata. Be careful.

Another vibration.
I read it out loud:

Rita and Casey got married in Canada. In Halifax.

30

Appendix II

THEIA MANIA:

"SOME ENCHANTED AFTERNOON."

The first time I saw Billy I was ten years old, fatherless, awkward, and directionless. I was up in North Jersey visiting my aunt, attending a freshman football game at DePaul against Hudson Catholic. Billy had just scored from twenty yards out, and he came back to the sidelines, and he took off his helmet.

I pity those who've never experienced what I felt at that precise moment. Something that's so marvelous, so extreme, so inexplicable, that the hapless poets have spent millennia trying to find a way to describe it. I was young Juliet looking at my Romeo, the little mermaid looking at her prince, Maria looking at Tony, Bella looking at Edward.

What does Shakespeare's Ferdinand say when he sees Miranda?

> *The very instant that I saw you, did*
> *My heart fly to your service.*

What are some of the useless words the writers use?

intoxication

madness

addiction

irresistibility

helplessness

instantaneousness

etc.

I wish that I had more time to explain this better than I'm doing. Trying to explain the inexpressible, the unexplainable. The ineffable. All I can do, the very best that I can do, is to admit that, at that sudden initial sight of my Billy, my life began. It now had "purpose." My heart was seized, and my mind was focused and single-minded.

No one has ever loved another human being more than I've loved Billy Kelly.

Yes, I know it's vain. I know it sounds self-important. I know it seems perfectly ridiculous that such a stupendous thing could happen to a silly ten-year-old girl.

But it did.

Billy, of course, was handsome, stunningly so, with dark sweaty hair, darker eyes, which proved to be black/brown, and Irish Kennedyish features, and, yes, a bit rough-edged.

In other words, perfect.

When the game was over (he'd scored once again, and DePaul triumphed 21-10), I told my aunt that I wanted to buy a coke before we drove back to her house. Then, quickly, I made my way down to the field, walked right up to him, and spoke.

When I think back on it now, it was only the *theia mania* that gave me the courage, the audacity, the fortitude. After all, I was a goofy, skinny, scaredy-cat, little nothing of a girl, with all kinds of inferiority issues, but I walked right up to Billy Kelly and I spoke to him. As if under a spell. As if it was my fate. My destiny. As if I didn't have a choice.

"Nice game."

Well, maybe it wasn't exactly Shakespearian, but the contact was made.

He looked down at me, still holding his helmet in his hand.

"Thanks, kid."

That was it.

It was over.

He didn't gush, but, at least, he reciprocated. He didn't blow me off, and he seemed to truly appreciate what I'd said.

He was polite.

Charming.

That afternoon initiated the rest of my life. My *real* life. A life dedicated to loving Billy Kelly until I was old enough that he could love me back.

Confiding in no one, I cyberstalked him for the next five years, followed every detail of his football career, created a scrapbook and a secret web file, and dreamed about him night and day. When one of the newspaper accounts of a game at Don Bosco referred to him as an "honor student," I immediately changed that part of my life. There'd be no more floating my ass through middle school. I needed A's. Nothing less. I needed to try and become what I thought he'd want me to be.

When he graduated, he got accepted at Johns Hopkins. I knew that he'd injured his knee in his senior year and college football was probably out of the picture. So I wasn't surprised when he took a more academic route.

Finally, it was time to take action. I was terrified, but it was time to move from my fantasies into the real world.

I'd been preparing for years.

Saving my money for years.

Even though I was only fifteen, I was an honor roll student, and I'd arranged for a tour of the Hopkins campus as a "prospective" student. I took the bus to Baltimore, rented a room at a Motel 6, and paid very close attention to everything my tour guide said. The campus itself seemed like heaven.

Later that night, I tracked him down at a party at Wolman Hall. It was a booze-only, rather tame affair, which I was glad to see. It was very preppy. Billy was now a second-semester freshman, wearing jeans, a navy Hoppy polo, and deck shoes. He also had a Dos Equis in his hand and lots of surrounding friends. I won't bother to describe how handsome he looked, but I have to admit that I was pretty spooked by all the pretty girls at the party, all of whom were older than I was, and some of whom were prettier than I was.

When I saw my opening, I walked over.

"I saw you play at DePaul."

"Was I any good?"

He smiled.

He was polite and personable.

Perfect.

"You scored twice. Against Hudson Catholic."

"That was a long time ago."

"I was ten."

He was both surprised and amused.

"Ten?"

"Yes, but I remember it well."

He seemed pleased.

We talked about his football days, which I actually knew much better than he did, about his family (an aunt), his major (history), and about lots of other stuff.

Including me.

I won't pretend that he fell for me like I'd fallen for him. That would have been impossible anyway. But he was definitely intrigued, and I believe, no, I *know*, that there was a definite attraction. Possibly romantic. Possibly sexual. I have no idea, and I didn't care. All that mattered was that he was interested.

I made sure not to monopolize him all night, and I also made sure to talk to some of the other boys.

Making sure he saw it.

When the party began to wind down, I told him to come and visit me in Cape May.

"I will," he said.

"When?"

He thought it over.

"I'll be heading north next month with my buddy Sonny. Maybe I'll convince him to make the stop."

"Great. I'll send you a text with my info."

"Great."

Then I walked away.

Walking on air.

Of course, I really wanted to wrap my arms around his neck and kiss him on the mouth, but I knew I'd have to be careful. Slow and normal. I'd been planning to marry the boy for five years, and absolutely *nothing* and *no one* was going to get in my way.

31

Carlito's

RUTGERS WAS WINNING 42-40 at the almost-end of the first half. They were playing Michigan State, and the lead wouldn't last for long.

What the hell was Rutgers doing in the Big Ten anyway?

That's a rant for another day.

The don was sitting at his favorite table near the restaurant's only TV screen, watching intently. He was surrounded by a group of expensively dressed dagos, including his oldest son, Vinny Ravello, whom I'd called earlier tonight from Stone House.

"I'd like a word with your father."

"I'm not sure he'll want a word with you."

Thirty-nine days ago, I was standing next to Vinny's younger brother, Eddie, when he was gunned down at his limo place on Pennington Street. I knew Eddie growing up in Paterson, and we were "friends" of a type. The type that a law enforcement type like me could be with the youngest son of the most powerful mobster in North Jersey.

As for Vinny, we were always wary, at arm's length, but always polite and respectful. There were times, like now, when I needed the Ravellos, and there were times when they needed me.

Vinny Ravello, ever the tough guy, realized that he'd come off a bit too dismissively, so he tried again.

"What's up, Jack?"

"Just a word. Three minutes."

I could hear him smile over the phone.

"Are you asking for a favor, Jack?"

I admitted the truth.

"I guess I am."

"Can you come to Carlito's?"

"In the Ironbound?"

"Yeah."

"I thought your father never left Paterson?"

"His cousin owns the place, and they want to watch the Rutgers game."

"I thought he hated basketball?"

"Yeah, but I guess there's a bet of some kind."

Of course, there was.

"I'll be there by halftime."

Which I was.

I was sitting at a table for two in the back of the crowded Carlito's watching the beach girl drink a caipirinha. We'd just knocked off a quick supper: ziti and ricotta for me, manicotti for the princess.

It was an Italian restaurant in a neighborhood famous for its countless Portuguese restaurants, and they knew how to mix up a decent caipirinha.

It was my suggestion when she asked, "Can detectives have booze on the job?"

"*You* can."

She took a sip.

It flowed over her tongue, and her eyes got big, and she smiled like a teenager.

"Yum!"

"Yeah, I thought you might like it."

I'd spent three years in Newark at Seton Hall Law, and I knew the Ironbound well. *Real* well. I loved the place. It was mostly Lusophone, of course, but other-ethnic as well. My law school pals and I would eat over here all the time, at the very best restaurants, mostly Portuguese, but also Brazilian, Ecuadorian, Mexican, Spanish, and even one that no longer exists run by a family of Cape Verdeans.

I still love the ambiance, the food, the people, and the music. Portuguese fado. Brazilian samba. But now I was in Carlito's listening to Jerry Vale, singing lightly in the background, and I couldn't complain. Who doesn't like Jerry Vale?

"What is it?" she wondered.

"Lots of sugar, lime, ice, and eighty-proof cachaça."

"What's that?"

I didn't know how to explain it without a diagram.

"Something like rum, but different."

She smiled again.

"*That* really clarifies things!"

"If you don't get too loopy, I'll buy you another one."

"I'll buy my own, Mr. Big Shot."

Then Little Miss Big Shot knocked off her drink and raised her hand for the waiter.

"While you're getting blotto, I think I'll do what we came here to do."

I walked over to the Ravello table, wondering about the don's "bet" on the game. Wondering if it was the kind that he couldn't actually lose.

Probably not.

When Vinny saw me, he got helpful, alerting the old man.

"It's Jack. Jack Colt."

The don turned around in his chair and looked at me. Maybe it would be more accurate to say that he looked *through* me. Which he always did. He was sixty two years old, with a face that was indelibly impassive, wary yet hyper-confident, with alert never-miss-a-thing blue eyes.

He didn't bother to say, "What do you want?" he just waited. So I told him.

"I'm working a cold case in Cape May that has nothing to do with you or any of the families, and I need your permission to talk to someone."

"When have you *ever* asked my permission to do anything? Or your uncle for that matter?"

He spoke about my uncle like he was still alive. Maybe it made him feel younger. Whatever the case, I liked it.

"I'm asking now."

"Who's the 'someone'?"

"Your niece, Isabella Borelli."

"I thought you said it didn't have anything to do with me?"

I ignored him.

Three nights ago, when I was reading over Pavese's suspect list, the name "Borelli" clanged some kind of bell in my brain, but it didn't dawn on me until this morning exactly why. When Eddie Ravello and I were wiseass kids on the streets of Paterson, he sometimes mentioned his "loser Shore cousins." The "Borellis."

The don was waiting, so I explained my problem.

"I don't think she'll talk to me unless you tell her to."

He smiled. Almost.

Allowing Vinny to speak for the family.

"Yeah, she's a piece of work, all right."

The don thought it over.

"Is she involved?"

"She knew the dead girl ten years ago."

"Is she a suspect?"

"No."

Which was a lie.

I don't lie much, almost never, and I'm not very good at it. But I've noticed that lying to thugs and gang creeps and mobsters gets easier all the time.

"Fine, work it out with Vincent."

"Thank you."

There was no response, and he turned away.

I stepped back from the table, and Vinny came over, and we "worked it out."

I never mentioned the six heads staring at the Passaic River. What was the point?

Then I walked back to my worn-out, exhausted, slightly lit caipirinha girl.

32

Borgata

I LIKE CASINOS.

I'm not sure why.

Gambling's for saps, and the places are all lights and glitter. But, for some reason, I like the endless jingle, the all-day nocturnalism, and the preposterous sense of both fun and the hope that "springs eternal in the human breast."

Atlantic City might be in a slump these days, and a few of the other casinos have boarded up, but the Borgata was having no such problems. It's the biggest hotel in the state of New Jersey, with over two thousand rooms, and it's the top-grossing casino in Jersey.

Unfortunately, it also has an unpleasant whiff of the Cosa Nostra. The back-to-back heydays of Nucky Johnson and Little Nicky Scarfo were long gone, but not so long ago, the casino got nailed. Twenty-three losers were arrested for running an illegal underground sports book out of one of its exclusive poker rooms. They'd raked in at least twenty-two million before the hammer came down, and most of those arrested were either Borgata staff (supervisors, dealers, bartenders) or various capos and soldiers associated with Philly mob boss, Skinny Joey Merlino.

Oh, well.

Tonight was a Saturday night, and the place was hopping. Since clocks are verboten in casinos, I checked my watch. It was 2:16 a.m., and my sleepy gal Friday was out in the Explorer resting her pretty head.

It had been a long day, and she hadn't been sleeping much since the "Edward Colt" murder.

I headed for the poker room, the largest in Atlantic City, with fifty tables, but my cell wiggled inside my suit jacket pocket.

Good.

I'd been waiting for this, which meant that Nonna was up way past her bedtime.

Good.

It was Nonna's Izzy report:

Isabella Borelli (age 26, croupier):

She seems to have been the "loose end" of the Nikki/ Rikki circle of teenage friends. A bit more "wild" than the rest of them, getting into a bit of cop trouble in high school. Shoplifting twice. But she was still "very nice," easy to get along with, and a good friend. She also had serious inferiority issues, always thinking of herself as the "skank" of the group, but, in my opinion, she looks kind of cuteish in the old photos with all that wild black hair.

Her father (James) worked as a mechanic at the Cape May ferry, and her mother (Maria) initially stayed at home with the five kids. When the father died, when

Izzy was eight, her mom started working at Gloria's Hair Salon on Bank Street, and Izzy joined her there, part time, during high school.

As you somehow figured out, she's closely related to the Ravellos, being the niece of Don Ravello, who's her mother's older brother. The Borellis are clearly a wing of the Ravello "family," but I can't find any indication that Izzy's father, Jimmy Borelli, was ever involved in the family "business."

I also can't find anything about a boyfriend back then. Or a girlfriend either. She was a good friend of Tommy Garrison, and maybe that caused some friction between Izzy and Nikki. But I have no idea. You should check with Rikki.

After high school, Izzy worked for two years, full time, at Gloria's Salon, then she seemed to vanish. It's no wonder that Edward Colt couldn't find her. It also seems that she cut off all her earlier ties with Cape May. (Her mother moved back to Paterson about eight years ago, into the Hillcrest District in the Second Ward.) At some point, Izzy also surfaced in Paterson, working at the Magic Hair Salon on Ellison Street for five years before ending up as a well-paid poker dealer at the Borgata. Surely, her uncle set her up. While still in Paterson, she was arrested twice for assault (I've got no details), but the charges quickly went away and nothing happened.

I know that I always give you a hard time, John, but be very careful around Don Ravello. I know too many stories. Tread lightly, and keep that pretty beach girl away from it all.

Sometimes you don't realize how dangerous you are.

Love, Nonna

I wish the old goat was here so I could contest her uncalled-for "dangerous" remark. Sure, my *job* is dangerous some of the time, but I don't think that *I'm* dangerous. Not in the abstract.

After all, I'm just doing my job.

A pretty girl approached.

I can always smell a hooker. They smell like STDs. But this one's scent was confusing. Maybe my sinuses were clogged.

"You having a good time?"

"More than I need."

She got the message.

She was wearing a diaphanous blue mini with blueberry lipstick and blue spikes to match. Wearing just enough clothing to keep the management from asking her to leave, which was the last thing they wanted since they got a cut.

In AC, as in Vegas, *everyone* got a cut.

Maybe she could be helpful.

"Where's Izzy Borelli tonight?"

"The high-stakes poker room. Upstairs."

"Thanks."

"Yeah, thanks for nothing."

I went upstairs and found the right room. I told the guy who was "clearing" the big-spenders at the door that I'd been sent by Don Ravello to give a message to his niece.

It made him nervous.

"You want me to call him? I've got him on speed dial."

That made him even more nervous, so he offered a compromise.

"Why don't I let you in, and you wait till her break?"

I didn't like the idea.

"When's that?"

He checked his watch.

"Ten minutes."

"All right."

He stepped aside, and I stepped inside.

The place reeked of stale sweat and jacked-up air-conditioning. The "buy-in" was probably ten thousand or so. There were two well-heeled and well-dressed black guys at the table, along with some rich guy from the Middle East, and two overweight honkeys. All they needed to complete the cliché was a couple of cowboy hats.

And a beautiful dealer.

No problem with that. She sat there in the midst of them, running the show like Queen Dido before Aeneas docked at Carthage.

Whatever had happened during the past ten years (and it wasn't surgical), Izzy Borelli was *anything* but the local skank. She was wearing a super-tight red dress that accentuated everything important, including the stupendous mass of barely-tamed black Italian hair and her voluptuous lips, redder than fire-engine red. Speaking of fire, her sexual thermometer was stuck on max, and I assumed that the guys at the table had anted up more for the opportunity to sit close to the hottest number in Atlantic City than for the unlikely opportunity to poker their way to a few thousand extra bucks.

She looked like every young woman wants to look. Like the young Claudia Cardinale. If you don't know who that is, check Google Images.

You know something else?

(Pardon the digression.)

I never really liked the word "hot" to characterize a female. It always seems demeaning somehow. Or maybe it's just too overtly sexual for a prude like me. But I defy anybody to go to the Borgata high-stakes poker room, look at the dealer, and come up with a better word.

Izzy looked up from the table and looked at me like she was looking at trouble.

Actually, I was thinking it was the other way around.

Flawlessly, she continued her dealing, then she shut things down for a break. The morons at the table groaned in unison, although I don't think they were aware of it, as she arose from the table, standing above them like Dido ascending the pyre.

When she tried to duck out a side door, I cut her off.

"Get lost, pal," she said.

As if she said it a lot.

Time was tight.

"I've come from the don."

She didn't believe me, but she didn't want to take a chance.

"Prove it."

I dialed Vinny.

Thank goodness "made" guys like Vinny never go to bed.

"Little Miss Toughass is giving me a hard time."

"Put her on."

I handed my cell to Izzy.

She listened and mellowed a bit.

"You sure about this, Vin?"

She listened some more.

"All right," she agreed. "Give my love to the don."

It was nice to see her giving her love to somebody.

She looked at me, suspiciously.

Superciliously.

"Follow me."

I did what every guy in the Borgata wished he could do.

I followed her.

We went through the side door, into a small empty poker room, and she turned around and looked at me.

"What do you want?"

"Who's this?"

I handed her the motor vehicles photo of Billy Kelly. The picture spooked her.

"I'm not talking about that."

"I've also got the don on speed dial."

I lied.

She thought it over and decided to be impressed.

"Who the hell are you, anyway?"

"Jack Colt. I grew up with Eddie and Vinny."

She looked at me closely, finally realizing who I was.

"Then why are you bothering with a forgotten cold case in Cape May."

"Rikki hasn't forgotten."

She melted.

Not really melted. Thawed.

"How is she?"

"She's fine. She's also wondering how you are. So is Ronnie. So is Rita."

She seemed affected by old memories. Softened.

She handed me the picture.

"It's Billy Kelly. But I'm sure you know that already."

"I wanted confirmation."

"Is that it?"

She knew it wasn't.

"No, I'd like to know who you think killed Nikki O'Brien."

She laughed a why-are-you-wasting-my-time laugh.

"I don't have a clue. I never did. But I'm guessing you think it might be me."

"You picked up two assault raps in Paterson."

"That was just stupid girl stuff. Two bitches at the salon."

"If you had anger issues in Paterson, maybe you had them ten years ago in Cape May."

"I'd never hurt Nikki, or *any* of those girls. After it happened, and Rikki never came back to school, my life was over. A total mess. Eventually, I left town and never went back."

She was pretty convincing.

"Was Ronnie ever jealous of Nikki?"

"No, that's a stupid question."

"Was Rita?"

"Not that I noticed."

"What about Rikki?"

She looked at me like I was an idiot.

"That's perfectly ridiculous. They were exactly the same person. *Exactly.* Hell, they were probably lesbians."

"Were you?"

"Of course, I am. Isn't it obvious."

In New Jersey, sarcasm is de rigueur.

"Any other dumb questions?"

"What about Tommy?"

She laughed.

An honest laugh.

"Tommy wouldn't hurt a fly."

"Didn't you two once have a 'thing'?"

She scoffed a "No."

"But you were close, right?"

"I was a skank back then."

She said it as if it explained everything.

"I doubt that."

I waited some more.

"Besides, Tommy was much-too-much the goody-goody boy for me. I thought he was perfect for Nikki."

"So who did it, Izzy?"

"*You're* the hot-shot detective on TV all the time, you tell me."

"I'm working on it."

"Are we done?"

"Yeah."

"Thanks for the memories, Colt. I won't sleep tonight."

I believed her, and I felt sorry for her.

"I'm sorry."

"Yeah, maybe you are."

A few minutes later, I stepped into an empty elevator and hit the button for the main floor. Just before the doors shut, two toughass-slickass-looking guidos got into the elevator. They took their positions, one on my right and one on my left, as I got a grip on my Blackout, from a specially tailored pocket inside my suit jacket.

A half hour ago, to make things easier inside the casino, I'd left my Colt and my holster in the back seat of the Explorer.

"Don't shoot anybody," I said to the sleepyhead in the passenger's seat.

"No promises," she said, with her eyes shut.

But I still had my Streetwise Blackout, which is perfectly illegal in New Jersey and a number of other states as well.

Within the ensuing silence, the three of us stared forward, mindlessly staring at our reflections in the elevator doors.

They were big guys, probably gym goons, and I wondered why they were after me.

Maybe one of them was Izzy's squeeze?

Maybe they were here to escort me out the front doors.

Maybe everything would be fine.

Not likely.

Then guido number one reached over to the panel and hit the stop button.

Damn.

I turned to the other guy and immediately crushed his shades into his face, which, given his response, must have been quite painful. Then I knelt down, avoiding the grasp of the button pusher, and I zapped him right in the groin area. Yeah, I know that I said earlier that I'd never hit a man in his "man region," but this was different. It wasn't a punch, and it wasn't a strike.

I didn't have to touch a thing.

The Streetwise Blackout fits comfortably into your palm and weighs about seven ounces, but it packs a punch. Over five million volts, leading to severe electroshock and neuromuscular incapacitation, immobilization.

Along with a world of pain.

I like tasers a lot. It's easier than any kind of physical combat, and a lot less messy than a handgun. But what I really like about tasers is watching the saps squirm around on the ground, jerking all over the place. Pain, spasm, and helplessness. It's a nice combination for goons, predators, and thugs.

Mr. Button was now on the floor of the elevator doing a lot of wiggling and squiggling, and I was quite disappointed that I couldn't watch the entire show.

I stood up straight and looked at the other guy who was trying to remove his now-crumpled frames and bits of plastic lenses from his bloodied forehead, while simultaneously staring down in disbelief at his squirming co-thug. Guys like that make me sick. They knock around anyone they're told to knock around, but as soon as the tables turn, they all look shocked.

Like, hey, *that's* not supposed to happen to me.

So I hit him with five million volts. Into the side of his neck, as direct as possible into his nervous system. Soon he was down on the floor, imitating his tough guy pal, and I hit the "stop" button, and we glided down softly to the first floor.

Just before the doors opened, I looked down at my travel companions.

"This is for the ones who can't fight back."

Then I zapped number one on the top of his head, which, if he had any brains, would have scrambled them against the walls of his thick skull. Then I zapped number two on his right hip, which I suspected would induce some especially interesting "hippy shakes," but I couldn't stick around.

I wanted to get back to the Explorer.

And the girl.

Besides, I felt naked without my Colt.

33

Explorer

Saturday, March 28th
34°

EARLIER, I'D PARKED the rented Explorer in the far reaches of the Borgata parking lot, so Rikki could catch some shuteye. I was hoping that the caipirinhas would help her fall into la-la land before we drove back to Paterson.

It was a coolish late Saturday night, actually early Sunday, and the chill was bracing. Especially after escaping a really badass beatdown by two guys who specialized in the activity.

When I was fifteen, my uncle gave me my first stun gun. He showed me how to use it, and how to conceal it. And how to be prepared for the worst.

Always.

"If you do what you say you want to do, Jack, they'll be coming for you."

Which was the reason why I wasn't off in some AC hospital with contusions, cuts, and broken bones.

Because the old man had prepared me for the worst.

But, tonight, the worst was yet to come.

I saw the orange glow.

Off in the distance.

Then the flames.

I had no doubt that it was the rented Explorer, and I rushed across the mostly empty parking lot. The entire front of the Ford was engulfed in red metastasizing flames, as if someone had poured gasoline all over the front of the car, then ignited it.

I couldn't see Rikki. I was unable to see anything inside the car. Given the intensity of the flames, I knew that the side doors would be useless. I pulled out the key fob and hit the liftgate button.

Nothing happened.

When I got to the back of car, the flames had almost engulfed the entire vehicle. Through the darkness of the back window, through the smoke and the fire, I thought I could see Rikki trying to crawl towards the liftgate, away from the flames at the front of the car.

I kicked beneath the rear bumper under the license plate. Nothing happened, but it was the only hope I had, so I kicked it again and again. Four times. Finally, the liftgate released and slowly opened. I reached into the heat and the smoke of the furnace, grabbed her by the shoulders, and yanked her out of the vehicle, doing my best to ease her fall down to the ground. Then I picked her up and quickly carried her away, about two hundred feet away, waiting for the tank to explode, waiting for the bullets in my Python to start flying in all directions.

"How bad is it?"

She looked herself over. She was definitely scared, but she was also an ETM, and she did her best to switch into professional mode.

"Not bad."

I could see some burns, some red, some black, and I dialed 911.

Suddenly, the tank lit up the Borgata parking lot like a Hollywood special effect.

I was thinking to myself, what if she was still inside?

I assumed that she was thinking the exact same thing, but I was wrong.

"Guess what I got?" she said.

With a smile.

I looked down and saw my weapon in her right hand. The Python my uncle gave me when I was twelve years old.

"I felt it when I was crawling across the back seat. I thought you might like it."

She seemed very pleased with herself.

34

AtlantiCare

Saturday, March 28th
34°

WHAT KIND?"

I was standing in the emergency room at AtlantiCare Regional. Rikki was sitting on a gurney, with an extra-large bandage on her right forearm and a smaller one on her right temple.

The doctor knew what I meant.

"First degree."

"All of them?"

"Yes."

I know a lot about burns. Too much. Somehow Rikki had escaped with just a couple of first degree burns.

The young doctor turned to Rikki, unaware that she was a nurse, a paramedic, an EMT.

"You probably won't blister much, but it'll definitely hurt. Maybe five to ten days."

Rikki nodded.

"I'm a lucky girl."

"From what I've heard, you're lucky to be alive."

Rikki pointed at me.

"The big goof yanked me out of the fire. I'm surprised he didn't dislocate my shoulders."

The doctor smiled.

"Is that it?" I asked.

I was trying not to be impatient. But I was. Whoever had just tried to kill her would know that we were now at the hospital, and I wanted to get her out of here.

Immediately.

I looked at Rikki.

"We're leaving."

The doctor was cautious.

"I'd like to keep an eye on her for an hour or two."

"Not tonight, doc."

I took Rikki's cellphone and handed it to the young doctor.

"Put this in your lost-and-found. We'll come back for it in a day or two."

It made him nervous.

"Somebody's trying to kill this girl," I assured him.

He got the message, and he looked at Rikki.

"The lost-and-found is located on the first floor. Check at the reception desk."

I looked at Rikki, she stood up immediately, and we left. Out in the parking lot, I broke into a random Lexus, disabled its GPS, and hot-wired the engine.

Rikki watched in silence.

Until I was done.

"I've never been an accessory before."

I opened the passenger door.

"Let's go for a ride, wiseass."

Forty-six minutes later, I put her to bed in the Beach Haven guest room.

"Sleep," I said.

"Yes, sire," she said. But she was ready and willing. I'd propped her arm nicely, and she was asleep as soon as she hit the pillow.

But I was certain that I'd never sleep tonight. I put on my sweats, double-checked the locks, and went out the back of the house to the beach.

The beach cottage on Long Beach Island was my uncle's "safe house," which *no one* knew about, except Roxs.

Not even Luca. Not even Nonna.

Many times over the years, it had come in handy, and I knew that Rikki, for the moment, was perfectly safe.

I sat down in the pre-dawn chill and stared at the blackness of the ocean. I'd been doing a lot of that lately.

I remember that one of the Cousteau's, maybe the grandson, once pointed out that more is known about the surface of the moon than about the oceans, only five percent of which has actually been mapped. He also pointed out that twelve human beings have bounced around the moon, but only two human beings have visited the Mariana Trench.

The sea was calm tonight and dark tonight. Black with bits of gray and silver. Hardly Homer's "wine-dark sea," which I've never actually seen, in either the day or the night.

Maybe no one has.

When I was a boy, I read the epics, quickly becoming an *Iliad* and Agamemnon enthusiast, but I naturally wondered about that "wine-dark" business. So I read up on it. A bunch of experts thought it was simply a poeticism of some kind. Others thought that the Greek soil was alkaline enough to shade their wines to blue. Another guy wondered about a possible "red tide" of red-colored algae. Another one claimed that red dust lurking in the atmosphere created red sunsets which affected the color of the water.

Another one said, "Hey, look, the guy was blind, so what the hell would he know about the color of anything?"

Of course, no one seems to really believe that the guy was blind.

Who knows?

Who knows why I was wondering about it.

Maybe I was trying to push the fire from my mind.

Maybe I was trying to push the girl from my mind.

Maybe I was trying not to remember that the pretty young woman presently sleeping in my cottage was sleeping in the same bed that Roxs slept in.

Several times, in fact.

Maybe I was just tired and stupid.

III

New Jersey is a social experiment. Pack in as many humans as you can, as tight as you can, and see what happens.

— Thomas C. Colt

35

Beach Haven

I WAS SITTING on the couch.

Since I couldn't sleep, I decided to go over Pavese's "suspect list," as once amended by Edward Colt (aka Billy Kelly), for the thousandth time:

> *Ronnie Miller – victim's best friend, age 18*
> I doubt it.
>
> *Isabella (Izzy) Borelli – victim's friend, age 16*
> I doubt that too.
>
> *Rita Rockingham Sehorn – victim's friend, age 15*
> Who knows? Why not?
>
> *Billy ?? – Johns Hopkins student, age 18?*
> I doubt he killed his brand-new wife.
>
> *"Sonny" ?? – University of Maryland student, age 18?*
> I doubt it. He was probably already back in North Jersey.
>
> *Judge Richard O'Brien – victim's father, age 42*
> I don't see it.

Rikki (Erica) O'Brien – victim's twin sister, age 16
No way.

Tommy Garrison – victim's boyfriend, age 17
The guy still piques my interest. Despite what
Izzy says, despite what *all* of them say.

Kitty Walsh O'Brien – victim's mother, age 34
It's not hard to list her as a definite POI, but if she
really wanted her daughters dead, why'd she wait
ten years to go after the second one?

Mitchell Kain – witness on the beach, age 48
As much as I'd love to bag this jerk, I'm not
buying him for any of it.

Like Edward, I'd also emended the list, adding:

Deborah Rockingham – mother of Rita, age?
Since Rita's mother is dead, she couldn't be
chasing Rikki all around New Jersey. But that
doesn't mean that she didn't kill Nikki ten years
ago.

Which raises the possibility of multiple killers.

Which raises the possibility of colluding killers.

Which got me thinking again about the age-old jealousy/envy
problem. How people tend to conflate the two. Just for the hell of
it, I texted an old lawyer buddy and asked for his brother's phone
number.

It came back immediately, so I dialed.

"Yes?"

I recognized Bret's voice because he sounded just like his brother,
or the other way around. Bret Buchanan was a hot-shot literary guy
from Wayne, who was up in Canada writing a novel. I didn't know
him that well, but he knew me.

"It's Jack Colt."

I sensed surprise in his non-response, and since there was no sense making small talk with a guy I hardly knew, I got right to the point.

"Iago wasn't 'jealous,' and neither was Othello. Othello was just an idiot who got duped into becoming a 'green-eyed monster,' and Iago was an envious little creep. Right?"

"Right."

"Thanks."

"No problem."

I hung up.

People confuse the two words and use them interchangeably. But envy's the desire (or lust) for something you don't have. Like covetousness. But jealousy is the desire to keep whatever one already has.

Like a lover.

Deborah Rockingham wasn't "jealous" of Nikki O'Brien. She was envious. She wanted everything that Nikki had—that Rikki had—for her own daughter.

Of course, that didn't mean she killed anyone.

Rikki came into the room, still a bit drowsy, having slept in her clothes, except for her shoes and socks. Looking perfectly lovely in her rumpledness.

"Who took off my socks?" she smiled.

"Who do you think?"

"Did you think about taking off anything else?"

"No."

Which was true, although I'm not sure why.

Satisfied with her wake-up flirting, Rikki sat down on the couch like Cleopatra on her barge.

"I like tea, but not coffee."

"Good for you, now get up and get it."

I nodded in the direction of the kitchen, and the pretty barefoot girl smiled again.

"What's on the agenda?"

"Nothing for burn victims. You're staying right here."

She wanted to pout, but she understood.

"You can use the beach, but keep the sand off those bandages."

"Whatever you say, Dr. Colt."

"You look like Nicholson in *Chinatown*."

An obvious exaggeration.

"Incorrect. Jack's bandage was on his nose; mine's on the side of my head."

"Close enough."

"You got a bathing suit?"

"There's no swimming with first-degree burns."

"Thanks again, John Colt, MD."

I decided to answer her question.

"I think we've got one."

"Of course, you do. For all the girls you bring to your love shack. All your girlfriends."

She liked teasing me. Especially since she knew she could get away with it.

"I don't have girlfriends."

"I thought Jack Colt didn't lie?"

It was good to see her being so silly again, especially since, a few hours ago, some lunatic had tried to burn her to death.

"I had a girlfriend once," I admitted. "Now she's gone."

"Where?"

"California. As far as possible."

"Is it *her* bathing suit?"

"Yes. It's in the closet on the back porch. There's also some towels, but no flip-flops."

"I hate flip-flops."

I was impressed.

"I hate them more," I insisted.

"I doubt that. They're ugly, gross, and dangerous. Pumps for white trash. Trailer Park Stilettos."

"Don't hold back."

She laughed.

"I didn't know beach girls could be so supercilious."

"Only regarding matters of the beach. Besides, I'm an EMT who's spent a lot of time in the emergency room."

I waited for the coming dissertation.

"Every year, there are thousands and thousands of flip-flop injuries. Tendonitis, cuts, bruises, sprains, strains, scrapes, broken bones, stubbed toes, and overpronation."

"Anything else?"

"Yeah, did I mention they're ugly?"

36

Pompton Lakes

Sunday, March 29th
40°

I LIKE BREAKING INTO houses.

This one was a little brick with bright-yellow trim on a side street in Pompton Lakes, ten miles from Paterson.

It was Rita Sehorn's house, as neat and orderly and lawyerly as its owner. Comfortable, but somehow lacking both warmth and comfort.

I busted in the back of the house and snooped through each and every room, finding nothing of interest except that I was finding nothing of interest.

Even inside her baby blue bedroom.

The other bedroom had clearly been her mother's. On top of the bureau, there was a large framed picture of the two of them. Smiling. I had the feeling that nothing had been touched or moved since the mother had died five years ago.

Like a shrine.

A memorial.

I sat down on the bed and read Nonna's report:

Rita Rockingham Sehorn (age 25, prosecutor):
  Maybe you know all this stuff by now.
  She was born in Cape May where her father (Andrew) was the postmaster and her mother (Deborah) was a nurse at Cape Regional. Apparently, Rita was good at everything except sports: straight A's and lots of extracurriculars, like dance, cheerleading, and the Legal Club. She went to the same kindergarten, grammar school, and high school as the O'Brien twins, so I guess she knew them for most of her life. They seem to have been great friends—along with Ronnie and Izzy.
  The summer after the murder, she and her mother move to Pompton Lakes. I'm not sure why. Rita managed to complete her final two years of high school in a single year at Pompton High and ended up valedictorian, making a speech that was mostly a tribute to her friend Nikki.
  (I've got a copy if you want it.)
  After graduation, she matriculated, pre-law, at Drew University, eventually transferring to McGill in Montreal. I'm not sure why. In Montreal, she met Casey Sehorn, a criminal justice major from Edmonton, and they married a year later in Halifax, honeymooning on Prince Edward Island.
  A year later, they moved back to New Jersey, moving into the Pompton house with Rita's mother. Rita soon matriculated at Rutgers Law in Newark. I guess she was commuting. As for Casey, I'm not sure what he was doing at the time. Eventually, for some reason, the marriage fell apart, and Casey left. Then, when Rita's mother was visiting relatives in Washington State, she collapsed and died of a heart attack. She was buried in the family plot in Tacoma, Washington.

*In the aftermath, Rita finished up her law degree
and interned with Judge Ralph Carlson at the Newton
Courthouse. Last year she was fast-tracked into an
Assistant Prosecutor position in Sussex County.*

*She's got no police trail of any kind, and she lives
alone in the little brick house in Pompton Lakes.
Apparently, she's a hardworking and well-respected
prosecutor.*

I'm still trying to locate Casey Sehorn.

Be careful, knucklehead.

Love, Nonna

I dialed myself.

"Colt's badass detective agency."

I tried a conciliatory approach.

"Is this the sweetest grandmother in the entire United States of America?"

"Yes, it is."

Despite the alacrity of her response, I could tell that she was a bit nonplussed, a word I don't get to use that often.

"I wonder if you could check a few things."

"I'll see if I can fit it in."

I ignored her.

"Call all the storage facilities in the area surrounding Pompton Lakes. Tell them you want to know when your contract runs out."

I wondered if I was about to get blasted for telling her how to do her job, but she let it slide.

"Fine."

"It might be under Rita's name. Or maybe her mother's name, Deborah Rockingham."

"Or it might not exist at all, right?"

"Right."

"Anything else, Mr. Bossman?"

"Yeah, find Casey."

"I already did."

I waited for at least several eternities.

"He's out in the Gap. At least, he was out there a few years ago. I'll text you the address."

"Someone's the best."

"She certainly is. You have yourself a lovely day."

She hung up. Usually I'm the one who hangs up on people, so it was useful, every once and a while, to experience what it felt like.

I left Rita's house, leaving from the front door, and looked around her quiet suburban neighborhood. There were two self-absorbed kids sitting next door under their front-yard tree. A boy and a girl, maybe a brother and a sister, maybe ten years old or so, diddling away on their stupid cellphones and ignoring each other.

I walked over, towering above them.

Like the tree.

The little girl looked up.

"Did you guys see the old lady today?"

I gestured at Rita's place.

I don't know why I had this nagging notion that maybe the grave in Tacoma, Washington, was empty. That maybe Deborah Rockingham was alive and well. I had absolutely no tangible reason to make such an assumption, but, as Rikki once pointed out, I'm the suspicious type.

"What old lady?" the little girl said.

"Doesn't an old lady live next door?"

"Just the lawyer lady. Mrs. Sehorn."

Having completed her neighborly obligations, she refocused on the hyper-addictive little box in her hand.

"Why don't you two brats get up off your asses and play some sports?"

They both frowned simultaneously, didn't bother to look up, and hoped that I'd go away.

I did.

37

French Hill Inn

X ANDER WAS SITTING at a table in the back, right where he always sat, right next to his mousy little girlfriend, who always sat on his right.

He was a criminal without a criminal record, and we always met at the French Hill Inn in Wayne, New Jersey, which was now calling itself the Taphouse Grille. Back in the Roaring Twenties, nearly a hundred years ago, the French Hill Inn was a very shady and sketchy roadhouse/speakeasy with lots of illegal booze, illegal gambling, and illegal working girls.

On the night of February 17, 1926, two New Jersey State Troopers went inside to investigate the previously raided roadhouse. Trooper Charles Ullrich was shot dead in the head, declared DOA at St. Joe's in Paterson, and Trooper Charles McManus was knocked unconscious with a baseball bat, suffering permanent mental impairment. The shooter, Sam Alessi, who was also the co-owner, along with his baseball bat wielding bouncer, James "Slam Bang" DeLuccia, were both subsequently arrested and convicted.

The place should probably be a memorial today, but the contented Taphouse customers, eating their Steakhouse Burgers and Braised Short Rib Pot Pies, didn't have a clue.

Maybe it was better that way.

Maybe Xander knew, maybe he didn't.

History wasn't a strong point these days, especially with his generation, but he had other abilities. It was true that Nonna was a hell of a looker-upper and a finder-outer. She'd been a librarian for a billion years, and my uncle had trained her about the legal and criminal side of things. But Nonna was no criminal herself, never doing anything that might be illegal, like hacking, which was why people like me needed people like Xander.

The kid had dropped out of Eastside High when he fully comprehended his computer capabilities. His old man, Constantine Demetrios, who owned the Haledon Diner, just shrugged about it. Xander was now twenty-four years old, and, on the surface, he was hardly the computer geek stereotype. He wore, as he always did, an ordinary brown business suit with a dark brown tie. Nothing hippieish. Nothing gothish. Not even anything quirkyish. The kid was always polite; he had a seemingly normal, nicely dressed girlfriend; and they both seemed perfectly well-adjusted. No drugs, no booze, no arrests.

But the kid was a bloody terror in cyberspace.

When he saw me approaching, he stood up and put out his hand.

"Mr. Colt."

As we shook hands, Marcie stood up.

"You remember Marcie?" he said.

"Of course."

I shook hands with his little cutie, and we all sat down.

Xander, like me, was never much for small talk. He had the full report in a little manila folder in front of him on the table. Next to his lemonade.

He knew it all by heart.

"Her account was shut down four years ago. A year after her death in Washington State."

He was talking about Deborah Rockingham.

"For fifteen years, subsequent to the death of her husband, Andrew Rockingham, she received monthly payments, forwarded automatically from the personal account of Richard J. O'Brien of Cape May, New Jersey, in the amount of $1,500."

He sounded like an accountant.

"She lived on O'Brien's stipend, along with her husband's governmental pension of $2,122.16 a month, plus her own personal annuity of $956.22 a month, arranged through the Cape Regional Medical Center, where she'd worked as a maternity nurse for fourteen years. At her death, being only fifty-one years old, she wasn't yet eligible for Social Security benefits."

"Anything else of interest?"

"Not really. Except for the O'Brien deposits."

I nodded.

"Does it make sense to you?" he wondered.

Xander never stuck his nose into the gritty details of my investigations, but he wanted to make sure that he'd been useful.

"Yes, I believe it does. Good job."

Yes, the respectable judge had seemed "above reproach" to Detective Pavese—and everyone else—but his ex-wife had told me in the Pines:

"He keeps *all* of his women comfortable."

I guess Deborah Rockingham was one of "his women."

Xander handed me the manila file.

"It's all inside."

"Thanks. Send me your bill."

The kid never liked to talk about money, as if it was beneath him, and I respected him for it.

When I stood up, the two lovebirds stood up, and I went outside to my latest rental, a black BMW 3 Series.

Once I was comfortable in its soft leather seats, I called the burner phone down in Beach Haven.

Rikki picked up.

"The bathing suit fit nicely."

"That makes my day. Is someone behaving herself?"

"Yes, I think she is. She went into the water up to her waist, keeping her bandages perfectly dry, and now she's cool, refreshed, and damp."

Was she flirting again?

I hoped so.

"It's March," I pointed out.

"So what? I swim all year round."

"I don't believe it."

"You're smarter than you look."

I reminded myself that there was an actual purpose to the call.

"Tell me about Deborah Rockingham."

"I've *already* told you about Mrs. R. About everybody else for that matter."

"Tell me what you forgot to tell me."

She thought it over.

"I can't think of anything new. Rita hung at our place a bit, but we never went over to hers. Her mom was always a bit coldish and standoffish. Not really hostile, but not really welcoming either. So I never saw her that much. Besides, she was a nurse at Cape Regional, and she kept funny hours."

"Did your father know her?"

I could sense a shrug in Beach Haven.

"Maybe. Maybe in passing."

I left it right there.

"Is she a suspect."

"Everyone's a suspect."

"Even me?"

"We've been through this before."

"But I thought detectives were supposed to *eliminate* suspects?"

"I prefer to be open-minded."

"Yeah, that's a very believable word for the likes of you!"

"Goodbye, Rikki."

"When are you coming back?"

"Goodbye, Rikki."

"I'm going back to the couch to lie down and read some Shakespeare. I was reading Act 3, Scene 2, of *The Winter's Tale*, when some law enforcement type rudely disturbed me."

"Goodbye, Rikki.'

I hung up.

38

Delaware Water Gap

Sunday, March 29th
44°

S HE VANISHED."

"You want to elucidate?"

We were standing on an isolated dirt-road offshoot of Old Mine Road, overlooking a spectacular view of the Delaware Water Gap, where the Delaware slices beneath the Kittatinny Ridge of the Appalachians. Behind the young trooper, across the deep and long Gap, was distant Pennsylvania. Behind me was the burned-out shell of a small rustic home at the western edge of the Worthington State Forest.

In truth, *all* the views of the Gap are quite "spectacular," which is why George Inness came here in the 1860s and painted numerous landscapes, and why there's always one of his pictures hanging at the Met.

Trooper Hank Turner, wearing his sharp gray/blue uniform, with neat yellow patches, was probably in his mid-twenties, boyishly handsome, diminutive, energetic, athletic, and, fortunately for me, talkative.

He elucidated.

"Mr. Sehorn popped up at the Hope Station one day and told me that his girlfriend was missing. He said her name was Pamela Johnson, and that they shared a home off an isolated trail from Old Mine Road. He said she'd been missing for two days, but he didn't have a picture, and his description was pretty generic. When I started asking questions, he got edgy and evasive and left."

"What kind of questions?"

"Stuff like, 'Where does she work?' which he shrugged off and said she was 'in between' jobs. He wasn't very convincing."

"What else?"

"He said there was no problems in their relationship. 'Absolutely not.' He was emphatic about that, but when I asked him if he could send me a picture, he said, 'Sure, I'll see what I can do.' But who says something like that if he really thinks his girlfriend is missing?"

I had no answer.

He continued.

"Then he stood up, thanked me, and left the station. He never bothered filing out a missing person's form, and he didn't even take my business card."

"Is this him?"

I showed the Trooper the DMV picture of Billy Kelly.

"Yeah, that's him, but maybe ten years ago."

"What was he like?"

"Polite. Actually, very polite, but wary as well. I might even say he seemed 'spooked' about something. As if he didn't know what to do."

"Did you ever hear from him again?"

"Never."

"Did you follow up?"

"A little bit. I did a routine check on Pamela Johnson and found nothing."

"Nothing?"

"Nothing at all. Except that the house behind you had been purchased in her name. In cash. From the previous owner. Two days after the guy's visit at the station, I was up in the area, so I stopped at the house, but Sehorn wasn't at home. Neither was his car. The very next day, I heard the news about the fire. It seemed as though the guy had simply vanished. Just like his girlfriend."

"Anything else?"

"Yeah, I contacted the guy's estranged wife, a lawyer over in Sussex County. She seemed both surprised and concerned, but she had no idea where Sehorn might be, and she said that she'd never heard of Pamela Johnson."

Turner turned, looking down at the far base of the Gap, at the Delaware River.

"Maybe they're down there somewhere. In the river."

39

U-Store Storage

Sunday, March 29th
45°

A s I mentioned earlier, I like breaking into houses, but storage facilities can be fun, too. You never know what you're going to find.

I disabled the lock, then slid up the garage-like door. The unit, on Route 23 in Wayne, was registered in Deborah Rockingham's name, and it was as neat and perfectly clean as Rita's brick house.

Which, of course, had once been her mother's house.

I turned on the light and shut the door behind me. In the far left corner, there was a wooden file cabinet, and in the far right corner, there was a matching cabinet. In between them, there was a handsome wooden desk with a wooden chair.

As if waiting for me.

The cabinet on the left was the "Billy" cabinet. It was full of countless old newspaper articles about William Kelly, beginning when he was a freshman in high school, playing football at my alma mater, DePaul High School, right here in Wayne, New Jersey. There were various programs, photographs, and Facebook printouts, all neatly organized. Chronologically. There was also a meticulously crafted scrapbook lying flat in the bottom drawer. There was a particularly interesting file about a "prospective student" trip to Johns Hopkins ten years ago, and another file containing a handful of wedding pictures.

There were exactly seven wedding pictures, each of them including just the bride and the groom. No one else. Rita, looking buoyantly happy, in a pleasant off-the-rack white dress, holding a small bouquet of colored flowers, and Billy, wearing a neat navy suit, and looking equally content.

The right-side cabinet was mostly empty. It contained the "life" documents of the lives of Rita and her mother. Birth certificates, wedding licenses, insurance policies, medical records, financial records, etc. In the bottom drawer, there was a red wig and a small pack of letters bound with a rubber band.

I sat at the wooden desk, within the airless, moteless, windowless room and tried to put it all together. Two lives. A mother and a daughter. Plus Billy. Sitting directly in front of me, on the top of the desk, was a upright wooden frame containing two pictures side-by-side. One was a grainy selfie of a little girl, maybe ten years old, standing next to a slightly older kid in his football pads holding his helmet. She was smiling like she was the happiest girl in the world.

The second picture, taken by someone unseen, was a young woman and a young man at a high school football game. She was maybe twenty years old, and he was a bit older. He had his arm around her. Affectionately. They were both smiling, and Rita was again smiling like she was the happiest girl in the world.

It was, I suppose, the perfect symmetry of her life.

The kind of ordered, exacting, and appropriate symmetry that life affords to very few of the rest of us.

I removed the rubber band and read the first letter from

Ginger Addison to Edward Colt. It was short and sweet, actually bittersweet, dated last January:

> *Dear Edward,*
>
> *You don't respond to my texts, but I've found you anyway, and I'll continue to write you a letter every single week until you respond.*
>
> *Your disappearance, without a word, has left me empty and devastated. Yesterday, I started crying at work, at my desk, uncontrollably. Everyone was very nice about it, but I was ashamed. I was pathetic.*
>
> *I don't know why you're in Cape May, New Jersey, but I'm waiting here, where we had so much happiness together, waiting for you to, at least, tell me why, if not to tell me that you're coming home to fall within my arms again.*
>
> *All my love, Gee*

I counted the letters. Ten total. Ten days. I skipped to the last one, also short, also sad:

> *Dear Edward,*
>
> *I can no longer write these letters. It's too painful. I know that I'll have to accept the fact that what I thought we had—and what I thought it meant for our future— was just a delusion on my part. Maybe that's why you left. Maybe you saw within my eyes the desperation of "last hope," of "last chance."*
>
> *I just wish you that you had told me face-to-face. Your refusal to communicate, in any way, has made a horrible situation even worse, but, having admitted all that I've already admitted, I still wish you the best, nothing but happiness, and I continue to leave my door always open.*
>
> *Love, the one who loves you*

Life's a bitch.

I don't say that in any way that might seem dismissive or belittling of the pains of life. It's just a fact. Life can be hard, especially on those who love without getting it back, those who crave love yet never really find it.

Ginger Addison, whoever she is, hurts my heart.

I texted Nonna.

> *Find out whatever you can about Ginger Addison, 218 Cranberry Street, Harrisburg PA, 17101, who was Edward Colt's girlfriend last year. Thanks.*

I made sure to add the "Thanks."

My cell vibrated immediately, which was way too fast. It was the California girl from California. I read her daily "new" text, then I reread the one from a month ago:

> *I'm standing in Furnace Creek, Death Valley, the hottest place on earth, were they shot the famous* Twilight Zone.

Meaning the episode called "The Lonely."

I dialed the judge, and he picked up immediately, surely worried about his daughter.

"I know about you and Deborah Rockingham."

There was apprehensive silence.

"*Everything*," I assured him.

There was more silence, so I waited. Sometimes, I can be pretty good at waiting.

"Does Rikki have to know?"

40

Stone Tower

*A*NY PROGRESS?
   Still working on it.

The old Jesuit seemed pleased.

You don't need to check up on me, Jack.

He was probably right. He might have both feet in the grave, but he was also indestructible. Even though he looked like he hadn't eaten in a year.

Like a cadaver.

You're the only Colt left.

Except for you.

Actually, there were lots of multifarious Colts roaming around out there, but only two of us remained from our particular branch of the tree.

He remembered something.

What about Edward Colt?

His real name was William Kelly.

Then why'd he call himself a Colt?

I don't know. But let's face it, if you've got to be somebody, why not be a Colt?

Yeah, why not?

There was a momentary pause.

Who's the girl?

What girl?

The one in the Beach Haven cottage.

How do you know about Beach Haven?

I know about all kinds of stuff. I've been around for ninety-eight years.

How did you know about *her*?

He smiled.

I refuse to answer on the grounds that I might incriminate myself.

I smiled. In spite of myself.

Did you ever consider the fact that you might know too much? Too much about everything? That it might be clogging up your brain?

Yes, but it hasn't killed me yet. Stop ducking the question. Who's the girl?

The sister of the dead girl.

The twin?

Yes.

Did she kill her sister?

No.

Are you sure?

Yes.

He thought it over. In the same way that he might have evaluated a theological fine point regarding Liguori vis-à-vis Aquinas.

Has she fallen for you yet?

I think so.

Have you fallen for her yet?

I think so.

I qualified.

As much as possible under the circumstances.

He looked at me like I was an idiot.

You're an idiot.

I had no counterargument.

Yes.

You need to straighten out your life.

Yes.

Yes, yes, yes.

He was frustrated, a condition rare in his previous ninety-eight years.

I'm getting tired of praying for you.

I said nothing.

It's wearing me out.

41

Appendix III

*P*ERQUISITION:

I'M DOOMED TO TRY and describe the indescribable.

Billy had vanished off the face of the earth.

Probably thinking, I'm sure, that he was the primary suspect for the murder that I'd committed.

With all my daughterly wiles, I'd managed to manipulate my manipulable mother into moving to North Jersey.

"Why, honey?"

"It's too sad here."

Meaning Nikki's death.

"Why Wayne?"

"Because it's where Aunt Helen used to live, and I always loved it there."

The good news is that nurses can get a job pretty much anywhere, and my mom was already tired of her situation in Cape May.

"All right."

So we found a little brick in Pompton Lakes, not far from Wayne.

So I could search for Billy.

Relentlessly, I talked to his friends, his teachers, his neighbors, and, several times, to his Aunt Rosaline.

"I honestly don't know, sweetheart. I really don't."

She was a lovely woman, but I didn't believe her. Despite her "honestly." Except for me, she was all that Billy had left in this life. After all, she'd been his surrogate mother since he'd been abandoned at birth.

"Please."

"I'm sorry, dear."

So I dove back into the web, googling every word and every name, first and last, in the English language that might lead me back to my Billy.

For over two years.

Then it happened.

"Sehorn."

One afternoon when his aunt was out of the house, I snuck into Billy's room. I'd been there many times before, and a few times I'd even slept in his bed. I already knew everything in the room by heart, but that day, as I lay back in his bed and looked at the far wall, I stared, once again, at what he stared at every night before he went to bed: a collage of photos and posters related to the New York Giants, his favorite football team, something I'd become a bit of an expert about.

And *there*, in the midst of Tittle and Huff and Simms and Carson and all the rest of them, was a photo of Jason Sehorn's pick-six in the 2001 NFC Divisional Playoff against the Philadelphia Eagles.

I suddenly realized that, for some reason, I'd never tried the cornerback before.

That night I initiated an intensive "Sehorn" search, and I eventually found a suspicious one in Canada, at McGill University.

His name was Casey Sehorn. He had a negligible web trail, and he was majoring in Billy's favorite subject: criminal justice. At the time, I was enrolled, pre-law, at Drew University in Madison, New Jersey, but the next day, I flew to Canada.

The day after that I "bumped" into Billy on campus, on the lower lawn, and he was very happy to see me. We immediately started hanging around together, and, eventually, we talked about Nikki's death. I was very supportive. Billy wondered if it might have been her old boyfriend, Tommy Garrison, and I encouraged the idea.

I took it slow, and I won him over.

It was wonderful.

In time, he fell in love with the one who loved him more than he could have ever imagined.

We married in Halifax, the most spectacular day of my life, in the history of the world, and we honeymooned on beautiful Prince Edward Island.

I'd never made love before, and it was everything that I'd been dreaming about for the past nine years.

Eventually, we moved back to New Jersey, into my mom's brick house in Pompton Lakes. My relationship with my mother was always good, always supportive, especially after my father died when I was five years old, especially since she had gargantuan guilts about spending so much time at the hospital working long shifts when I was younger.

As anticipated, she thought Billy was the greatest, and he thought the same of her. I enrolled at Rutgers Law in Newark, Billy (Casey) got a big-shot job at Ellis Security, and our lives were perfect.

Then it happened again.

It happened again.

Billy vanished off the face of the earth.

Without a word.

Without a note.

Without a text.

I cried, I searched, I cried some more. The police, of course, were perfectly useless, and all kinds of foul and creepy theories infected my disordered mind, mostly relating to Cape May.

For example, what if Tommy Garrison had tracked Billy down, thinking that Billy had killed Nikki, and killed my Billy.

That kind of thing.

Eventually, somehow, I learned to live with his absence because I *never* really believed that I wouldn't find him again. A few months later, my mother thought it would be a good idea for both of us to "get away for a bit," visiting relatives in Washington state. But I didn't want to leave New Jersey, not with Billy out there somewhere, so she went by herself. On the third day in Tacoma, I got a call from her cousin, Ellen, who told me that my mom had had a fatal heart attack.

It seemed inexplicable.

I was crushed into nothingness and perfectly inconsolable. Somehow, I boarded the plane, arriving in time for the funeral and the burial, but I remember very little of those numbed-out days on the West Coast.

Once again, I entered a familiar state of suspended animation.

Back home in New Jersey, I was completely overwhelmed with loss and loneliness. Eventually, to keep myself from going insane, I started looking for Billy again.

Searching.

Maybe I could find him a second time.

It took me two long years, but I finally found him in the Gap.

His credit cards were long since blank, as was any kind of web presence, or anything else. But, this time, he didn't change his name, and I found a "C. Sehorn," living off Old Mine Road, who'd purchased a used Chevy Malibu from a used car lot in Blairstown, New Jersey.

Why had he left me?

I had no idea.

Why had he left without a word?

I knocked on the front door of his little house.

When you knock on a door, you never know what's going to happen next.

Sometimes, you don't get what you expect.

When the door opened, I found myself looking into the face of my dead mother, looking, until she realized it was me, quite happy. Quite content. Looking rather pretty, I'd have to admit, for someone who was my mother, who was fifty-two years old.

Nothing was said.

Despite the pain, despite the discombobulation in my screwed-up mind, I somehow knew, almost instantly, that my husband Billy had run off with my own mother, who'd used her relatives to stage her death.

I fell down, collapsing to the ground, remembering little afterwards.

Somehow I ended up back in Pompton Lakes. I was reading the online obituaries for North and Central Jersey. Then I found what I was looking for in Somerville. A dead cop. His name, oddly enough, sounded familiar. Sergeant Bruno Vitelli. I remembered that Ronnie Miller had an uncle named Vitelli who was a cop.

Perfect.

I bought a cheap red wig, went to the reception at the Vitelli house, snuck into the main bedroom, and found the dead guy's service revolver.

The next day, I knocked on the front door again.

My mother opened the door, and I shot her in the face. It felt good. Earlier, on my drive to the Gap, I wondered if I would kill Billy too. I wasn't sure, but I didn't have to decide. He wasn't home.

I got my mom in the trunk of my car, drove down to the Delaware, waited until evening, tied on the weights I'd purchased at Home Depot, and dumped my mother over a cliff into the waters below.

She sank much quicker than I'd expected.

Then I went back home and tried to decide about Billy.

The next day, I went back, intending to give him another chance, fully intending to kill him if he didn't take it. But the house was smoldering, burned to the ground.

Once again, Billy had vanished off the face of the earth.

42

Beach Haven

Sunday, March 29th
38°

I T WAS TIME to tell her what I knew.

At least, what I *thought* I knew.

At least, most of it.

We were sitting on the Beach Haven couch in the dimly lit living room. It was three minutes before midnight, and she was wearing ridiculously baggy black sweats, which she'd obviously taken from the bureau in my bedroom.

She smelled like mango and tangerine.

I tried not to be distracted.

"Rita first saw Billy Kelly when she was ten years old, up in North Jersey, and she fell instantly in love with him. Yes, instantly. I know that ten year olds aren't supposed to fall into *that* kind of love, so I'll let you call it whatever you want. She was totally obsessed from afar, cyberstalking Billy, and she told no one how she felt, not even her mother.

"Ten years ago, when she was finally ready to act on her five obsessive years of meticulous planning, she took a bus to Baltimore, sat through a Johns Hopkins student tour, and somehow, somewhere on campus, encountered Billy, probably inviting him to visit her in Cape May.

"When he arrived, bringing along his friend Sonny, he took one look at Nikki on the promenade and decided, suddenly, that he wanted nothing else in life. I have to admit, I've wondered a good bit about what might have happened if *you'd* been there. How would he have reacted with the two of you there?

"It's a foolish and wasteful speculation.

"On the other hand, it's not too hard to imagine Rita's reaction. Take your pick: shock, outrage, exasperation, jealousy, hatred. All of the above. The very next night she incapacitated your sister, put her into the trunk of your Mustang, and drove it into the ocean. But it didn't help because Billy Kelly was gone. Most likely believing that he was the main suspect, which he *was*, he never returned to his home in Packanack Lake. In Wayne, New Jersey. Undeterred, Rita somehow convinced her mother to move to North Jersey so she could search for the one she loved.

"Eventually, she tracked him down. I have no idea how she did it. He was using the name Casey Sehorn, and he was studying at McGill University in Montreal. Rita immediately went to Canada, matriculated at McGill, found him on campus, and, within a year, they were married. The next year, they moved back to New Jersey, into her mother's house in Pompton Lakes. Maybe they were happy for a while. I have no idea. Then Billy left her, and her mother faked her death, and they ran off to the Delaware Water Gap together.

"The son-in-law and his mother-in-law."

Saying it out loud didn't make it any less crazy.

Rikki was stunned.

How could she *not* be stunned?

"They were lovers?"

"Yes."

I waited a moment, then continued:

"When Rita found out about the betrayal, she stole the Beretta after the funeral reception in Somerville, and, I assume, shot and killed her mother. I say 'assume' since the body's never been found. Once again, Billy hit the road and vanished, trying to hide himself under a second alias in Harrisburg, Pennsylvania, before coming to Cape May."

"To solve Nikki's murder?"

"I think so. I think he was now convinced that Rita had killed both Nikki and her own mother, and he wanted to close the case, exonerate himself, and put Rita in jail."

As Rikki was thinking things over, it seemed a good time to qualify everything.

"At least, that's what I *think* happened."

"Then Rita tracked down Billy one more time and killed him?"

"Yes. I think she probably confronted him, and when he rejected her, she killed him with the same Beretta. Then she discovered that he'd had a girlfriend in Harrisburg, and I think she drove to Pennsylvania and killed her with the same weapon. The one she put in Nikki's desk drawer. We'll know for sure soon, once we get the ballistics from Harrisburg. Her name was Ginger Addison."

The name didn't register with Rikki.

"Now Rita's after me?"

"Yes."

"Why?"

"Probably because you had three diner dates with Edward."

She shook her head in disbelief.

"*I'm* the one who told her about it."

I was surprised, but not astonished.

"At the courthouse?"

"Yes. I thought it was just 'girl talk.' She said she'd read about the murder of someone named Edward Colt, and I told her that I knew him a bit and that I even went out with him a couple of times. She seemed very sympathetic."

"Psychos often do."

"It's hard to believe, Jack."

"Murder often is."

She thought it over.

"I've alerted Dawson," I explained. "I have a feeling that she's gone totally off the rails."

"Why?"

"She's getting sloppy, which isn't at all like Rita. I think she doesn't care anymore."

"Suicidal?"

"Maybe."

My cell vibrated:

> *Your father's next, Rikki. Meet me at Antonio's tomorrow night at 10:30. You can bring Colt.*

Speak of the devil.

43

Antonio's

Monday, March 30th
38°

L UCA DECIDED to come down "just for the hell of it." His decapped-heads case was, as expected, going nowhere, so he took the day off and drove down from Paterson.

To help out.

He was sitting in the opposite corner of the mostly empty restaurant, sitting across a red-and-white tablecloth from a young Cape May cop, both of them dressed in casuals, finishing their entrees.

Dawson was also in the room, sitting by himself, always alert, sipping an after-dinner dark beer.

I was back in the far back corner, facing the front door, just like Wild Bill *should* have been sitting on the night Jack McCall shot him in the back in Deadwood. Across from me, dressed like Rikki in a dark "bob" wig, was another Cape May cop, young Jennie Ryerson who seemed quite excited, even delighted, to be the bait, the undercover decoy.

Maybe Deadwood was a cue to the universe. My cell vibrated,

and it was Roxs's daily text. Then I took a quick look at her text from a month ago, when she'd finished her cross-country tour, getting as far away from me as her little red Neon would take her:

> *Back home in Hermosa, Colt, roasting on the beach in*
> *my yellow bathing suit.*

"Anything important?" Ryerson wondered.

I shrugged.

"Nah."

I put my cell away.

Outside in the parking lot and a few key spots in the surrounding area, other local cops were sitting in unmarked cars, wired into the restaurant, on surveillance detail.

No one, of course, was really expecting Rita to drive up to the front door and walk inside with a Glock in each hand. But we couldn't just ignore Rita's demand, so it was a matter of wait-and-see.

As for the real target, she and her father were nearby and safe, waiting at the Cape May Police Station on Washington Street. This afternoon, when I was leaving Beach Haven, I told Miss Rikki, with absolutely no qualification, to "Stay put. *Right* where you are."

But two hours later, she called me with the bad news.

"I'm in Cape May, Jack. I rented a car and drove myself down."

"Why don't women ever do what I tell them to do?"

"Maybe you lack the necessary authority."

I was angry, but what could I do about it?

She made an attempt to justify herself.

"She's threatened my father, Jack."

"Yeah, so she could shoot you in the head, dumbbell."

It didn't make a dent.

"I need to be with my father."

I thought it over.

"All right, get your ass over to the police station, and I'll tell your father to meet you there."

"All right."

But she was curious.

"You setting up things at Antonio's?"

"I'm trying, but now I've got to worry about my bozo beach girl."

"Is that what I am? Am I your 'bozo beach girl,' Colt?"

What can I say? I love it when pretty women tease me and bust my chops.

"You're my pain in the ass."

"How enchantingly romantic."

"Just stay at the station until you hear from me later tonight. After nothing happens at Antonio's."

"Your wish is my command."

I hung up.

It always felt good to hang up on Ms. Sarcastic.

I finished my dessert, a house-specialty tiramisu, keeping a close eye on the front door and deftly fending off, as politely as possible, Officer Ryerson's over-eager questions about the "Little Girl Killer" case.

Which was another bloody mess I'd found myself sunk in the middle of about eight weeks ago, which seemed a lifetime ago, which I was trying to forget.

The ear bud got active.

"Male, maybe thirty, approaching from the parking lot."

Fine. Probably just a late-night customer. Or maybe someone coming to pick up one of the staff.

I put down my spoon and watched as Tommy Garrison walked through the front door and looked around the dining room. He was dressed casually in white jeans and a navy sweater, but he seemed agitated, and I didn't like it.

He saw me.

Then he saw the fake Rikki.

Then he walked across the room in our direction.

There was something hateful in his eyes, so I took hold of my Python, which had been lying, ready and waiting, on the empty chair at my right.

"Gun!"

It was Luca.

Who was now standing up with his weapon pulled.

Tommy paid no attention. He seemed, oddly enough, focused on me.

Not on the fake Rikki.

"You bastard!" he said.

I really didn't want to shoot the guy, but I figured that I'd have to. As he started to lift his weapon, I was ready with mine.

"Don't do it, Tommy," I warned him, but he paid no attention.

A shot rang out.

Luca's slug came through his right shoulder and stuck in the back wall of the restaurant. Tommy slowly slumped to the floor, staring down, incomprehensively, at the blood gushing out of his wound. Officer Ryerson kicked his weapon away.

He looked like a stunned little child.

I bent over and pressed his wound with one of Antonio's bright-white linen napkins.

He was in too much shock to feel his pain.

"What the hell was that?" I asked, even though I had a good idea.

He didn't answer.

Then Dawson came over and took charge.

As we waited for the ambulance, Dawson got him talking. It was pretty much what I expected.

Rita had called him and somehow convinced him that *I* was Billy Kelly, and that I was the one who'd killed Nikki. As absurd as it sounded, I wasn't completely surprised. This poor dumb sap had spent the past ten years of his life wondering why his girlfriend had dumped him for some college kid she barely knew, dreaming all the time about killing the kid for killing the love of his life.

A sad story.

Like so many other stories.

But where did it leave me with Rita?

Luca was wondering the same thing.

"What's the bitch up to?"

I shrugged.

"I don't know."

We all knew the "meeting" at Antonio's was a diversion of some kind, but to what end?

My cell vibrated.

It felt uncomfortable.

"Yeah?"

It was the judge.

"She's gone."

He was terrified.

"What do you mean, 'she's gone'?"

"Ronnie called the station, and Rikki talked to her for a minute or so, and then she vanished."

I was too incredulous to respond, so he offered his lame excuse, both for himself and for all the cops at the station.

"She said she needed the ladies room."

As Dawson and the EMTs were prepping Tommy for his trip to the hospital, I told Luca to go to the police station, talk to the father, and see what he could figure out.

It was obvious that Rita had somehow lured Rikki away.

To somewhere.

But where?

I had an idea.

44

Sunset Pavilion

COULD THIS BE the place?

The southmost end of Second Avenue was dark and deserted. There was no one on the jet-black beach, no one inside the Sunset Pavilion.

I checked "around" the pavilion. All four sides.

Underneath.

Nothing.

No one.

Maybe I was wrong.

I was counting on Rita being Rita.

She always seemed determined to find a demonstrable order within her disordered life. Some kind of symmetry. Wouldn't she believe that it was perfectly appropriate to kill the one sister where she'd once killed the other sister?

Maybe I was thinking too much.

Maybe I was hunching too much.

I looked down the beach toward the ocean. The beach was coal-black under the faint moonlight, and the ocean was even blacker.

The jetty was the blackest of all.

Maybe I should check the jetty?

Nikki had died there, in the waters just off the southernmost edge.

Not on the beach.

Not on the pavilion.

I looked at Second Avenue again.

Nothing.

Dead silence.

Then I started across the beach towards the ocean.

I wasn't looking forward to it. No one wants sand in his shoes, especially me, a Paterson city boy. But it was March, and it was cool, and the sand was harder than usual, and I didn't sink as deep as I would have in the middle of the summer.

Regardless, I hated it.

I made my way along the north side of the jetty, looking back at the pavilion every few minutes, seeing nothing.

No movement of any kind.

There was also nothing at the water's edge. Very carefully, I stepped on top of the jetty's slick black rocks to look over at the other side, dreading whatever I might find.

Nothing.

Just the waves, the wind, some sea foam.

When I looked back at Second Avenue, I saw her coming. She was carrying a gun in her right hand, passing the pavilion, and heading towards me.

It was Rikki.

Not Rita.

I have to admit, I was astonished.

What the hell was going on?

Carefully, I stepped off the ocean-sprayed rocks of the jetty.

When I looked back at Rikki, I could see another dark figure emerging from the side of the pavilion right behind her. Silently. It was Rita. She must have been watching me all the time, then taken her position when I went out to the jetty.

She was carrying a knife.

By the way, did I mention that I'm pretty much a dead shot? If I did, please forgive the repetition, but, whatever my copious faults in this world, I'm pretty damned good with a handgun, especially a Colt Python, the most accurate handgun in the world.

I lifted my weapon, and Rikki stopped in her tracks.

She was still unaware that someone was right behind her.

Did she really think that I was planning to shoot her?

I had no idea.

When Rita lifted her knife, she was still mostly hidden behind Rikki. I didn't have a shot.

So I tried something else.

"She's your sister!"

I called it out to the night, to the swirling sounds of the New Jersey shore, to the sounds of the splashing waves and the ocean breezes.

They both heard it.

They both hesitated, but I still didn't have a shot.

When her hesitation was over, Rita again lifted up her blade. I fired.

Shooting Rikki in the left thigh.

She immediately slumped forward to her knees.

I fired again.

Shooting Rita in the left shoulder.

I suppose the world would have been a better place if I'd

killed her on the spot, but I still had some questions and I still wanted some answers.

Rita fell in the sand behind Rikki, who turned around, saw Rita, and sized up the situation. Despite her own wound, Rikki, still down on her knees, moved over to Rita, tossed away her gun, tossed away Rita's knife, and began putting pressure on her would-be assassin's shoulder.

An EMT to the last.

When I got there, I called 911 and looked down at Rikki's leg.

"You're bleeding," I said rather stupidly.

She looked up for a moment.

"Yeah, some idiot shot me in the leg."

"It'll heal," I said.

Then she went back to work on Rita, who lay out on her back, seemingly catatonic, on the sin-black sand beneath the mitigating lights of the moon.

Rita's eyes suddenly came alive for a moment, and she looked up past Rikki, directly at me.

"I hate you, Jack Colt."

"I know," I said.

What else could I say under the circumstances?

Then she looked up at her half-sister.

"I hate you too, bitch."

Rikki didn't bother to say, "I know," because we all knew that she knew.

Rita's eyes shut. She went unconscious.

"Is she all right?" I wondered.

"It'll take more than a shoulder shot to kill this little psycho bitch."

45

Appendix IV

*D*ENOUEMENT:

I'M SITTING IN a rented car on Second Avenue waiting for Rikki.

[Drinks from a large white cup.]

I know she's coming.

I've got Ronnie in the trunk.

Actually, it was pretty easy getting her into the trunk. It was even easier than getting that dope Tommy Garrison to go to Antonio's tonight.

"It's the detective, Tommy."

"Colt?"

He was amazed, apparently too stupid to be skeptical.

"Yes, *he's* the one who once went to Johns Hopkins. *He's* the 'Billy' who killed Nikki ten years ago. Which is why, when Edward Colt started stirring up things, he returned to Cape May to cover his tracks."

"By killing Edward?"

"Of course."

It went back-and-forth like that for a while. He was easy to convince. He was still in love with Nikki, and he *wanted* to be convinced.

"You're sure, right?"

"Positive."

He believed me.

"He'll be at Antonio's tonight."

He'd made up his mind.

"Bring a gun," I suggested.

He hung up.

It was almost too easy.

Excuse me a minute.

[Drinks from her large white cup, then smiles.]

Hell, it's not half-bad.

Well, since this is the wrap, I suppose I should clarify a few things.

Specifically the first murder.

The one involving Nikki O'Brien.

One of my best friends.

Of course, ten years ago, I hadn't told my mother about the trip to Baltimore, so I asked Billy not to mention it to my pals in Cape May.

We were talking on the phone.

"Sure, no problem, Rita."

"We can act like we don't know each other."

"Sure, whatever you want."

Three days later, on a warm April afternoon, I was sitting on a bench at the beach with Nikki, Ronnie, and Izzy when two college boys strolled up the promenade, and I said, "Hello," and Billy came over with his friend trailing behind.

Billy wore tight new jeans, navy deck shoes, a Hopkins sweatshirt, and his *Rebel Without a Cause* windbreaker.

He looked perfectly perfect, and my lusting/loving heart slammed around in my chest. Happily.

For a few moments.

Then everything went wrong.

He smiled at me, nodding politely.

Then he looked at Nikki, with a look that made me sick to my stomach.

I was nauseous, instantly. Terrified and stupefied.

I honestly don't remember the rest of it too well. Just a bunch of fun kids fooling around on the beach, bowling a few games at Shoreline Lanes, and palling around on the Hawk Watch near the lighthouse.

At one point, Billy and Sonny went down to the beach so they could stand at what they figured was the "southernmost" spot in New Jersey. While they were gone, Nikki got a text, and I knew who it was from, and what it was about, even though she read it in silence and didn't say a word.

They were very discreet.

They were never obvious about the obvious attraction between them, and I was never obvious about the raging chaos within my heart, within my soul. For five years, I'd never told anyone about the all-consuming all-possessing love in my heart for someone whom I'd only met twice in my life, five years apart. I'm very good at self-possession, at an outward show of equanimity, at keeping my deepest thoughts and deepest feelings hidden from the outside world.

So I pretended to have a good time, saying goodbye to the boys just like all the rest of the girls when they hopped in Sonny's jacked-up red Camaro, but I knew it wasn't over.

I'm not sure how I knew, but I knew.

It was, I guess, the "look."

Billy's first look at Nikki, which was a bit like five years earlier, when I'd looked at Billy for the first time, as he stood on the sidelines with his football helmet in his hand.

The boys took off, heading for "North Jersey," and Ronnie, who was the oldest of the girls, dropped us off, one by one. Me being the last. I lived six short blocks from the O'Brien's house, and as soon as Ronnie drove away, I ran all the way to Beach Avenue, just in time to see the yellow Mustang pull out of the driveway and drive south alongside the ocean.

Billy was driving.

Nikki was sitting beside him.

I won't attempt to describe what I was feeling, because the pain was so completely numbing that I was barely conscious of what I was doing. Even to this day, I retain very little conscious memory of those terrible hours.

Twenty-eight long, black, interminable hours.

I found a hidden spot beneath a secluded tree on the O'Brien's front lawn, and I waited. All night. All the-next-day. Watching the judge and Rikki leave in the morning, then returning in the evening. I don't believe I left the spot once. Maybe I relieved myself. Maybe I walked around a bit. Maybe I even slept a bit, despite the April chill. Surely, I had nothing to eat. Somehow I must have texted my mother and told her that I was spending the night, then the next day, and then the next night, at Ronnie's house.

I suppose I was lucky that my mother was completely burned out, on a twenty-four-hour shift at the hospital.

I sat there in a kind of suspended animation. I suppose I was flush with hate, with fear, with self-pity, with bewilderment. I really don't know. But I do remember having absolutely no plan. None. Which was *not* at all like me. I *always* have a plan, objectives, strategies.

Not then.

Which made things worse.

Then she was back.

It was late on the second night, deep into the next morning, when I saw the yellow Mustang coming up Beach Avenue. This time Nikki was alone, which meant that she was driving the car, which was illegal, since she only had a driver's permit at the time, and the twins *never* did anything like that. They never did anything even slightly wrong, let alone break the law.

I met her in the driveway.

I must have looked terrible.

"Are you all right?" she asked.

I assured her that I was.

Despite her initial concerns about me, she was perfectly buoyant, almost exuberant, and I knew why, and I wondered if they'd slept together, and the thought made me want to kill her on the spot. Strangle her to death.

But she seemed glad to see me, and, for some reason, she seemed hesitant about going inside her house.

"What happened?" I asked.

"You wouldn't believe it."

I waited.

We were good friends. Close friends.

She decided to confide.

We sat on the back of the car, and she told me that she'd married my Billy.

Yes, married!

I was stunned and could do little but listen.

She told me how they'd fallen in love, how they gotten her worthless Piney mother to sign the consent form, how they ferried over to Lewes, and all the rest of it.

"Did you make love?"

The question seemed to take her by surprise, and she laughed.

"Not yet."

I slid off the back of the car as she thought it over. As if she'd somehow forgotten to do something that was perfectly obvious. Perfectly reasonable. I bent down and picked up a sizable flagstone from the edge of the front yard. Then I smashed her in the back of the head with all my might.

She tumbled off the back of the Mustang onto the driveway. Like a doll. Like a dead Barbie doll.

I got her keys, opened the trunk, and somehow managed to get her inside. I was never athletic like the twins, but I was strong for a girl my size. Then I got into her driver's seat, backed the car out of the driveway, and started driving south on Beach Avenue. Slowly. I'd only done a little practice driving before. After all, I was the youngest of all my friends, being only fifteen. So I drove along slowly, having no idea where I was going or what I was planning to do. Somewhere near the south end of the beaches, I remembered the Army Corps' mat-road near the jetty, and I drove the car across the beach, over the jetty, into the ocean.

As the car began to sink, rather slowly, I lowered the window and climbed out. Then I swam to the jetty rocks and watched the pretty yellow car sink into the black ocean. Then I thought of the one I loved, and I called out to the girl in the trunk of the sinking car.

"Where is he?"

There was no response, just the wind and the crashing waves. I stood up, numb and soaked, walked home, and collapsed into bed.

The next day, Billy was gone.

So there.

That's the Nikki killing.

As well as I can remember it.

[Drinks again, licking her lips.]

While I'm sitting here, waiting to kill her twin sister, let me have my final say before Miss Rikki arrives:

About love.

Love is something that everybody wants. Which some people have had in their past. Some in their present.

Some version of it. Some variant.

I understand that.

I really do.

There are *all* kinds of love, and I wish I could find a way to describe the love that I've had in my heart for the past fifteen years.

I must admit I'm quite fond of the word "transcendent."

I also like "stupendous."

I also like "something that *none of you* could even conceive of. Something that's far far beyond your grasp. Far beyond your limited capacity to comprehend."

To apprehend.

It's an all-life-consuming love and passion, every single minute of every single day. Which began with a single look. When a little lonely ten-year-old girl looked at a young thirteen-year-old boy.

Leading to:

Five years of meticulous obsessive preparation.

The murder of an unanticipated rival.

A three-year search.

A stupendous Canadian romance.

Betrayal.

More and more searching.

The murder of one's treacherous mother.

More and more searching.

Then begging:

When I learned that Billy was back in Cape May, using the colossally stupid name "Colt," after the kid that he'd once admired as a little boy playing football, I went to his house on Benton Avenue, and I begged him to take me back. I swore that I'd had nothing to do with my mother's disappearance, and I swore that I'd never hurt Nikki O'Brien. I begged him. Over and over. I humiliated myself. I actually got down on my knees, and when he said "No, I'm sorry, Rita," I went out to my car, thought about it for seven hours, and when he came back from his dinner date, I took the Beretta from my glove compartment, went around the back of the house, discovered him naked, rising from his swimming pool, and shot my love, who didn't love me anymore, in the forehead.

Then I went into his little house, saw the letters on his desk, and discovered that he'd had a recent lover in Pennsylvania.

Leading to:

The murder of some stupid woman in a place called Harrisburg.

Maybe I shouldn't admit this, but maybe it'll give you some indication of the depthless intensity of my love, but I very much enjoyed the idea of mutilating their pretty faces in some way: whether it was water bloat, or acid, or fire, or the knife. The faces of those who'd had the temerity to kiss the face of the one I loved.

Leading to:

Planting the gun in Nikki's drawer.

Still thinking, absurdly, foolishly, that I might be able to survive in a world without Billy Kelly.

Learning, at the Sussex Courthouse, exactly who was sitting across the table at the diner date that night.

Learning it, oddly enough, from the twin of the twin.

Learning also that her protector, the full-of-himself Jack Colt, was determined to talk to frizzy Izzy later that same night.

Aware, but, of course, not telling, where the skanky hair stylist was working down in AC.

Then purchasing two gas cans, filling them with Exxon, driving to the Borgata, driving around the ugly parking lot, endlessly, for over six hours, searching for the black Ford Explorer.

Setting it on fire, then watching the Paterson goon yank her out of the back of the car.

But, guess what?, I never give up.

Never.

Isn't it perfectly clear *just* how determined I am?

Then duping the dupe Tommy.

Then duping the dupe Ronnie, who's now duct-taped inside the trunk of the car.

And now, the coup de gras.

[Holds up a large knife.]

Now it all ends.

Judge me as you will, but know that I loved with a love that was more than even the poet's love, with all the latent powers of the cosmos. With a depth that's perfectly inconceivable to the likes of you.

Yes, *you.*

All you loveless saps and suckers.

[Reaches forward. The frame goes black.]

46

Memorial

I WATCHED FROM A DISTANCE.

I didn't want any pats on the back, but I felt I should be there.

If you love, or *might* love, the one, then you might also have loved the other one.

The dead twin.

If you love Rikki in some way, however that might be, then logically, inevitably, you also love Nikki.

It was eleven days since I'd shot Rikki and Rita, not that far from the memorial's temporary platform, and ten days since the ethylene glycol had killed Rita Rockingham Sehorn, with an excess of self-inflicted hematuria, convulsions, hyperventilations, and excruciating abdominal pains. By now, I'd read, numerous times, the transcript of the tape that she'd self-recorded in her room at the Queen Victoria on the night before I shot her, which was, naturally, the exact same room where Billy had stayed ten years ago, while Nikki was being murdered. I'd also watched, endlessly, the companion video that Rita had recorded, sitting in her rented car, contentedly drinking her antifreeze, before she tried to stab Rikki to death.

By now, everyone on the planet had read the transcript and seen the video, since she'd sent them electronically—her "apologia," lacking, of course, any remorse or apology—to acquaintances, old friends, reporters, news stations, websites, the Cape May Police Department, the New Jersey State Troopers, and the FBI.

Needless to say, it went "beyond" viral, and, once again, as a result, I was getting hyper-over-publicized. So much so, that I left Paterson and spent a few days in isolation at Beach Haven.

The local priest opened the memorial. His voice carried well over the various outdoor speakers, speaking to the large crowd in front of the temporary podium erected in front of the Sunset Pavilion.

Speaking, as well, to all the news cameras.

Speaking, as well, to me, hiding in my XTS, strategically parked on Beach Avenue, with the windows open, with a clear view of the distant proceedings.

I've never learned how to make accurate crowd assessments, but I'd put the afternoon crowd somewhere over two thousand.

When the priest was finished, Richard O'Brien spoke lovingly about his daughter. He broke down a couple of times, and, each time, Rikki stepped forward and put her arm around his shoulder.

I'm glad I wasn't in the room when the father had to explain to the daughter about the affair he'd had with Deborah Rockingham, twenty-six years ago, after his young wife had run off, back to her home in the Pines. However long their affair might have lasted, Deborah definitely ended up pregnant, and her postmaster husband apparently believed that his little baby girl, whom the mother named Rita, was his own child.

Did he ever know any differently?

I have no idea.

He died five years later of a heart attack. Maybe, hopefully, blissfully ignorant.

So the judge had to tell his daughter, which she already knew, given what I'd yelled out on the beach that night, trying to prevent Rita from driving a knife into her back. So maybe the two of them, the father and the daughter, sat down in their comfortable living room, and the father told her that, yes, one of her best childhood friends was actually her half-sister, and that the same half-sister had killed her twin sister, and that she also killed her brother-in-law (Billy/Casey/Edward), and then tried to kill her.

The father would also explain, I'm sure, as a kind of defense of his defenseless behavior, that he'd sent his former mistress, the mother of his daughter, her sister, monetary payments every month for the rest of her life.

Which probably explained why Deborah Rockingham was the only person in the entire town of Cape May who actively disliked the twins.

Who must have resented them.

Who was, here it comes again, jealous.

It was a conversation that I was glad to miss, but I was certain that Rikki was a lot tougher than she looked. She was also forgiving and understanding, and now, as they stood together on the platform, I felt certain that she'd already forgiven everything that the father had ever done.

After all, it was a good day for forgiveness.

A good day for remembrance of a beloved sister/daughter, but also for moving on.

It was exactly ten years since Nikki had been drowned and murdered off the rocky jetty that extended into the ocean behind the Sunset Pavilion, submerged in the trunk of her pretty "screaming yellow" Mustang.

Then Rikki spoke in what, I would have to say, was a most beautiful tribute to her missing sister, but, I would also have to admit, that everything that she said about Nikki sounded like she was talking about herself.

Describing Nikki as:

Sweet, funny, kind, mischievous, hardworking, goal oriented, etc.

Rikki's burn bandages were long gone, but maybe her left thigh was still bandaged beneath her lovely white dress. Maybe not. I did my best to miss the bones, which I did, and the gunshot was basically an in-and-out flesh wound.

Rikki stood on the wooden platform, the picture of equanimity and beauty, and I remembered that she'd kissed me thirteen days ago.

Then Ronnie spoke, then Izzy spoke, both in their own lovely ways, both in their own lovely white dresses. Even Izzy. Even Miss Powderkeg had somehow depressed her sexual thermometer for the memorial.

But let's face it, fifty-five percent of a bombshell is still a bombshell.

At one point, when Ronnie broke down and cried, the girls held hands, with Rikki in the middle, and it seem to make everything worthwhile.

The once-pretty silly teenage beach girls, now all pretty young women, no longer had to wonder what had happened to the friend they all loved so much.

There was, quite appropriately, no mention of Rita, or of any of her "doings."

As for me, I'd asked the judge to keep me out of it, but I still got mentioned several times as the person who'd "unraveled" the truth about the terrible tragedy.

For which I was grateful.

Over the past ten days, almost all the web reports and newspaper accounts invariably used the word "unraveled," and I had no problem with that.

When it was finally time for the mayor to "say a few words," I backed my Caddie out of its parking space and got the hell out of there.

Apparently, there was going to be some kind of scholarship in Nikki's name, and I was fine with that, but I had no interest in the bureaucratic details.

As I was driving up Beach Avenue, alongside the beach, alongside the ocean, my cell vibrated.

I wondered if I should ignore it, but I pulled over to the curb.

It was Roxs, the other beach girl.

> *I've applied for my old job at LAPD, listing you as a reference. Thanks.*

I wondered how many dumped boyfriends end up giving glowing recommendations for the one who's left them behind. For a job three thousand miles away.

I texted back my two-sentence-limit:

> *Prepare for the worst recommendation in the history of the world. Colt.*

I could hear her in Hermosa, reading my text, smiling, and saying, "Ha, ha."

Like a teenager.

47

The Fudge Kitchen

Y UNCLE, who was the font of all wisdom, once said:

> *The only reason to leave the city limits of Paterson, New Jersey, is to drive to Cape May and visit the Fudge Kitchen.*

He was right.

As always.

I was currently standing at the Kitchen counter picking out my favorites:

> *Chocolate (3)*
>
> *Chocolate Marshmallow (2)*
>
> *Chocolate Chip (2)*
>
> *For health reasons:*
>
> *Bing Cherry Vanilla*
>
> *Since variety is the spice of life:*
>
> *Vanilla Marshmallow*

The pretty girl behind the counter packed it up and wished me a "lovely day."

Let's face it, how could the day be anything else with nine sizable chunks of Fudge Kitchen fudge?

Who on planet Earth doesn't love sugar, butter, and milk, all magically blended and texturized?

I walked out the brick front of the store, beneath the blue awning, and saw her sitting on a bench waiting for me, still wearing her pretty white dress with a light blue trim.

Maybe I shouldn't have been surprised.

"Health store run?"

I ignored her, and she answered my unasked question.

"The reception doesn't start until five o'clock, so I snuck away. To catch you sneaking away."

I'd received an invitation to the post-memorial reception tonight at Congress Hall, but I expected to be back in Paterson long before it started.

When I didn't respond, we strolled up then down the Washington Street Mall, which was always packed tight in the summers, but was now sparsely populated in the coolness of April. It was still remarkably pleasant beneath the warming sun, and it's *always* remarkably pleasant walking along in the company of a lovely young woman.

"I knew you'd come," she said. "And I knew you'd hide yourself."

"I told you I'd come."

"You did."

It was the last thing I'd said to her ten days ago when my business in Cape May was finished.

We were standing in the hospital corridor. She had a bandage on her thigh, and she was limping a bit with a useless cane.

"What were you planning to do with that thing?" I wondered.

Meaning the gun.

Meaning the one she'd taken from her father's briefcase before she slipped out of the police station that night.

"I have no idea."

"Have you ever fired one?"

"No."

"Did you even know where the safety is?"

"No."

"Beautiful."

"All I knew was that she had Ronnie in the trunk of her car, and that I was going to get her back."

"Would you have shot her?"

"Definitely. If need be. If I could figure out how to do it."

It was time to go.

We both knew it.

"Will I see you again?"

"Yes."

"When?"

"I'll be back for the memorial. As long as I'm not part of it."

"Fine."

She leaned forward and kissed me on the cheek.

"Just the cheek?"

"Maybe there'll be more after Nikki's memorial."

I left the hospital, and now I was trying to leave her again. We walked to my car.

"What happens now?" she wondered.

"I have no idea."

I wasn't too good at this kind of stuff. Ask the girl in California.

"You're a mess, Jack Colt."

"Yeah, a ninety-eight-year-old priest said the same thing eleven days ago."

She laughed.

"So who's your problem?"

"You want her name?"

"Yeah."

"Roxanne."

"Where is she?"

"On a beach in California."

"Our beaches are better."

I didn't disagree.

"Is it ever going to work with Miss California?"

"I don't think so."

She leaned forward and kissed me on the mouth. She tasted even better than Bing Cherry Vanilla, and she put her arms around my neck and held me tight.

I did the same.

I thought I should say something.

"That was even better than the last time I kissed you."

"You've *never* kissed me, idiot. *I* kissed you."

She was right, so I kissed her again on her soft moist lips.

Eventually, we disentangled, and she looked at my shades, deep into my eyes.

"Goodbye, Jack Colt."

Then she turned around and walked away.

I won't try to describe how I felt.

Soon I was cruising up the Garden State, blasting the Boss, heading north towards the comforts of Paterson, wondering what the hell I was doing with my life.

William Baer, a recent Guggenheim fellow, is the author of twenty-two books including *New Jersey Noir*; *Times Square and Other Stories*; *One-and-Twenty Tales*; *Companion*; *The Ballad Rode into Town*; *Formal Salutations: New & Selected Poems*; *Classic American Films*; and *The Unfortunates* (recipient of the T.S. Eliot Award). A former Fulbright in Portugal, he's also received the Jack Nicholson Screenwriting Award and a Creative Writing Fellowship in fiction from the National Endowment for the Arts.

ALSO FROM ABLE MUSE PRESS

Jacob M. Appel, *The Cynic in Extremis – Poems*

William Baer, *Times Square and Other Stories;*
    New Jersey Noir – A Novel;

Lee Harlin Bahan, *A Year of Mourning (Petrarch) – Translation*

Melissa Balmain, *Walking in on People (Able Muse Book Award for Poetry)*

Ben Berman, *Strange Borderlands – Poems;*
    Figuring in the Figure – Poems

David Berman, *Progressions of the Mind – Poems*

Lorna Knowles Blake, *Green Hill (Able Muse Book Award for Poetry)*

Michael Cantor, *Life in the Second Circle – Poems*

Catherine Chandler, *Lines of Flight – Poems*

William Conelly, *Uncontested Grounds – Poems*

Maryann Corbett, *Credo for the Checkout Line in Winter – Poems;*
    Street View – Poems
    In Code – Poems

Will Cordeiro, *Trap Street (Able Muse Book Award for Poetry)*

John Philip Drury, *Sea Level Rising – Poems*

Rhina P. Espaillat, *And after All – Poems*

Anna M. Evans, *Under Dark Waters: Surviving the* Titanic *– Poems*

D. R. Goodman, *Greed: A Confession – Poems*

Carrie Green, *Studies of Familiar Birds – Poems*

Margaret Ann Griffiths, *Grasshopper – The Poetry of M A Griffiths*

Katie Hartsock, *Bed of Impatiens – Poems*

Elise Hempel, *Second Rain – Poems*

Jan D. Hodge, *Taking Shape – carmina figurata;*
    The Bard & Scheherazade Keep Company – Poems

Ellen Kaufman, *House Music – Poems*
    Double-Parked, with Tosca – Poems

Emily Leithauser, *The Borrowed World (Able Muse Book Award for Poetry)*

Hailey Leithauser, *Saint Worm – Poems*

Carol Light, *Heaven from Steam – Poems*

Kate Light, *Character Shoes – Poems*

April Lindner, *This Bed Our Bodies Shaped – Poems*

Martin McGovern, *Bad Fame – Poems*

Jeredith Merrin, *Cup – Poems*

Richard Moore, *Selected Poems;*
    The Rule That Liberates: An Expanded Edition – Selected Essays

Richard Newman, *All the Wasted Beauty of the World – Poems*

Alfred Nicol, *Animal Psalms – Poems*

Deirdre O'Connor, *The Cupped Field (Able Muse Book Award for Poetry)*

Frank Osen, *Virtue, Big as Sin (Able Muse Book Award for Poetry)*

Alexander Pepple (Editor), *Able Muse Anthology;*
Able Muse – a review of poetry, prose & art (semiannual, winter 2010 on)

James Pollock, *Sailing to Babylon – Poems*

Aaron Poochigian, *The Cosmic Purr – Poems;*
Manhattanite (Able Muse Book Award for Poetry)

Tatiana Forero Puerta, *Cleaning the Ghost Room – Poems*

Jennifer Reeser, *Indigenous – Poems*

John Ridland, *Sir Gawain and the Green Knight (Anonymous) – Translation;*
Pearl (Anonymous) – Translation

Stephen Scaer, *Pumpkin Chucking – Poems*

Hollis Seamon, *Corporeality – Stories*

Ed Shacklee, *The Blind Loon: A Bestiary*

Carrie Shipers, *Cause for Concern (Able Muse Book Award for Poetry)*

Matthew Buckley Smith, *Dirge for an Imaginary World (Able Muse Book Award for Poetry)*

Susan de Sola, *Frozen Charlotte – Poems*

Barbara Ellen Sorensen, *Compositions of the Dead Playing Flutes – Poems*

Rebecca Starks, *Time Is Always Now – Poems*
Fetch Muse – Poems

Sally Thomas, *Motherland – Poems*

J.C. Todd, *Beyond Repair – Poems*

Rosemerry Wahtola Trommer, *Naked for Tea – Poems*

Paulette Demers Turco (Editor), *The Powow River Poets Anthology II*

Wendy Videlock, *Slingshots and Love Plums – Poems;*
The Dark Gnu and Other Poems;
Nevertheless – Poems

Richard Wakefield, *A Vertical Mile – Poems*
Terminal Park – Poems

Gail White, *Asperity Street – Poems*

Chelsea Woodard, *Vellum – Poems*

Rob Wright, *Last Wishes – Poems*

www.ablemusepress.com

www.ingramcontent.com/pod-product-compliance
Lightning Source LLC
Chambersburg PA
CBHW031944010726
47493CB00007B/2070